Cover design by: Aaron Garms
Editor: Victoria Hyla Maldonado

© Copyright 2020 Romelia Lungu

All Rights Reserved

Protected with www.protectmywork.com

Reference Number: 85631910ized20S004

The characters and events portrayed in this book are fictitious. Any similarity to real persons, living or dead, is coincidental and not intended by the author.

No part of this book may be reproduced, or stored in a retrieval system, or transmitted in any form or by any means, electronic, mechanical, photocopying, recording, or otherwise, without express written permission of the publisher.

I dedicate this book to all the people who have had this kind of experiences, and to myself. If demons are out there maybe there is even a God or we have always been fooled.

INSOMNIA

We all have inner demons to fight, we call these demons, fear and hatred and anger. If you do not conquer them then a life of one hundred years is a tragedy. If you do, then a life of a single day can be a triumph.

- Yip Man -

CHAPTER 1

I am in bed, trying to sleep. I look at the ceiling and wait for the drugs to work so I can rest. I can't sleep without them. They take effect hard, and I have nothing to do but sit and look around the bedroom.

In front of me, I see a beautiful house. It has a red door. I stop for a few moments in front of the house. I don't know what I'm looking for there, and yet a strange force pushes me to open the door.

I open it and enter the house. I wonder how it is possible for such a luxurious home to have the door unlocked and the alarm turned off.

The TV is on.

I hear strange screams and the sounds of the TV. It's probably a horror movie. To my right, I see a couch. I approach and see a sleeping man. He is handsome, young, and full of life.

Does he live here alone?

I have no idea, and I don't care. If no one has woken up yet, it means he lives alone. On the walls are a few sconces that illuminate the room with a dim light. The

play of artificial light from the TV makes the atmosphere strange but pleasant.

I like weird things; they turn me on.

I'm approaching the man asleep on the couch. I smell his neck. He smells good. He wears only shorts. His chest is bare—such a strong and perfect chest. I stroke it with my fingernail.

Careful not to wake him.

He shudders, but doesn't wake up. He's probably dreaming of something erotic because his body arches and he moans lightly. I take advantage of the dream he's having, kiss him on the neck, and then trail my lips down his chest. My hands are on his body, and he doesn't wake up.

That gives me the courage to continue. His skin is so velvety that it excites me to the fullest. I want him, and I want to have sex with him. He's a bit too young, and yet I don't mind. I don't know him, but there is still something familiar about him.

He reminds me of the days when I was always in the clubs. I used to go out with my girlfriends, but I always ended up in the bed of a handsome and attractive man. Back then, I chose my sex partners carefully.

I was obsessed with sex and handsome men. What excited me the most was when I saw an elegantly dressed man who seemed very rich, with a lousy dwarf of a woman next to him. It excited me most when I approached him and she almost fainted when he pushed her aside.

At that time, I was a tall, sensual woman with long black hair. I was young without serious worries. I avoided staying home so I didn't have to sleep at night.

My long legs left every man breathlessly watching. I wore dresses as short as possible, leaving almost everything visible. Often, I even had women who wanted to spend a night with me. I refused nothing and no one, always willing to have new experiences.

I just didn't want to sleep at night so those awful nightmares wouldn't come. I'm not sure if there was ever a night in my life when I didn't have nightmares or fought the demons trying to control me.

Back in the moment, I undress and cling to his body. He is hot! I see a table by the couch. On it is a bottle of wine, a glass, and a corkscrew. The glass is half full. I lie down and take the glass and drink the wine from it. It is delicious; he evidently has good taste. He probably has the same tastes in women, too.

He is handsome, and I can't resist. I see that the wine bottle is empty, so I take advantage of his inebriation that may prevent him from waking up quickly. I'm going to have sex with him. He doesn't even wake up when I undress him.

I am feeling so horny.

I sit on top of him and move in a way that I didn't think I could. I feel good, so good; I can't stop. I haven't had sex this good in many years. I don't even know how I managed to resist as long as I did.

My husband is too busy with work, and when he comes home, he is too tired to have time for my carnal pleasures. Sometimes I miss the days when I had sex all the time with different people.

I don't know how long I have sex with him, but it is brilliant. I have multiple orgasms. His young penis arouses my long-dormant instincts. He wakes up just as I am starting to get dressed. He looks at me amazed, but also happy at the same time.

I lean back over him and kiss him passionately on the lips. His mouth still tastes of wine, and I get aroused again. I kiss him hard and stick my tongue in his mouth until he is out of breath. The smell of his body drives me crazy, and I want to have sex with him again.

I take advantage of his distraction and lift the corkscrew off the table. I stick it in his throat, continuing to kiss him so he doesn't make any noise. I kiss him until he stops breathing. His heartbeats become slower and slower and then stop. Blood flows from his mouth as I finish the kiss.

I step away from him a little and see the blood running down his chin from the corner of his mouth. I run my tongue over the still warm blood, and then I lower my face to his abdomen. I put my tongue in his navel and trail it up to his neck. He has a red streak of blood on his stomach.

I reach up to his neck where so much blood spills. I taste a drop from there, too. It is much better and sweeter than the blood that escaped from his mouth. I turn the corkscrew around his neck a few more times to make sure he's dead and leave.

It was an exciting night. I have never felt so sexy and attractive. I suddenly feel very relieved as I see a shadow leaving my body. I already know what it is, and I am no longer afraid. I have to wake up even if I want to stay in the dream for a while. I think I'll come back to him.

Demons of my mind
So full of their own kind
They never knew I had
A secret way inside.
Don't let too close
It's darker here
That's my demons lair
It's where my demons hide

- Yours cutely -

CHAPTER 2

My day starts as usual, with a lot of sadness and significant memory loss. I don't remember what I did the day before, and that worries me.

It always happens that way.

The first day after having a nightmare is very confusing for me. I still feel good today. I don't know why, but I'm in a very good mood as if I had an unforgettable night. I feel like I spent the night with a man. Not with my husband; he is always next to me in bed or at work.

I drink my coffee quietly on the terrace in front of the house, and I feel something inexplicable growing within me. I start to vaguely remember a handsome man. I put my hand to my mouth and begin to cry.

I cheated on my husband.

That's not possible! If he finds out, he'll kill me. But it can't be. I slept all night. It was probably just a dream. It must have been just a dream. Those pills drive me crazy and make me hallucinate. I think again that I should go to the doctor and tell him to change them for me.

I need something else.

I need something more substantial to make me fall asleep faster. Perhaps I've been taking them too long, and I have built up a resistance.

I continue my chores around the house like the perfect wife I'm trying to be. I can't work since I have insomnia so I took a vacation for a while and now let my secretary take care of everything.

I don't really care about the company my adoptive parents left me. I don't care that I'm a wealthy woman. It's all in vain. I have millions of dollars in my account, and I cannot find peace and happiness on this Earth.

In this world.

I feel like I don't belong in this world, and that drives me crazy. The nights have become an ordeal for me, mostly when I'm home alone. They have always been an ordeal, but in recent years, they have become more assertive.

My nightmares seem real.

Everything that happens in my dreams seems so real. Even though I am in my bed when I wake up, I still have the impression that what I do in dreams I do in reality. There are times when I feel like I'm not alone; there are times when I feel like someone is looking at me or someone is controlling my body.

Sometimes I see shadows coming out of my body, but I don't know if they are real or if I see them because of the pills I take to curb my hallucinations.

When I avoid sleeping at night, I try to sleep during the day when I can't manage to find something occupy me to stay awake.

I don't take pills to sleep during the day because I'm so exhausted that I just pass out. It doesn't even matter where I am at that moment. I just fall asleep without being able to control my eyes, so they don't close.

When I fall asleep during the day, I always feel a presence around me. I can open my eyes when this happens, but I can't move. Or at least that's how I feel... like I can wake up, that I am awake, but I think I'm sleeping. And there is total darkness around me.

I am so scared every time.

I can open my eyes, but I can't move. I can see around me, but I still don't see anything. I just feel an incredible sense of fear. I want to get up, and I can't. I am paralyzed, and the fear paralyzes me even more. I feel like someone, or something, is in the room with me.

Sometimes I feel someone's breath next to me; other times I see a shadow looking at me. I feel like the darkness will swallow me forever, and I can't do anything because I can't move and react in any way. I can only observe what's going on around me.

It's good that I can still use my eyes even if I often can't remember what I saw. I don't know what paralyzes me the most. Is it the incredible fear or the shadows I see? Is it the breath I hear next to me or the darkness trying to embrace me?

Every experience I have during the day ends the same. Before I wake up and move, I see a shadow above me, a shadow that looks like a demon. He is a black demon with horns on his head and a long tail. Every time, he appears above me and grabs my hands. He sits like that for a few moments and looks at me.

In those moments, I close my eyes because I'm afraid to look at that demon. I don't know what he wants from me, and I have the feeling that if I look into his eyes, I will never be able to wake up again.

After letting go of my hands, he disappears. The darkness disappears with it, and my fear disappears, too. Each time, I wake up crying and I need a few hours to recover.

I can't sleep at night.

I have the impression that everything is real. During the day, I can't sleep because I believe I will be stuck in the darkness forever. I'm exhausted, and I don't have the strength to fight anymore.

Sometimes I want that demon to take me and put an end to my suffering. Sometimes I don't want to fight and resist anymore, but still, something keeps me here. Something keeps me in this world to which I don't belong, and I don't understand why.

I don't even understand what keeps me in this world. I don't understand anything anymore, and I don't have the strength to ask questions. I don't even know where to look for the answers. I am afraid of myself, and I am fearful of everything around me.

Confront the dark parts of yourself, and work to banish them with illumination and forgiveness.

Your willingness to wrestle will cause your angels to sing.

- August Wilson -

CHAPTER 3

It's another night out of the dozens of nights. I've already lost track of the number. Sometimes I feel like I'm just going crazy, and sometimes it seems familiar to me. In twenty-four hours, I manage, if I'm lucky, to sleep for about six, but even these spans are getting shorter and shorter.

I'm already starting to feel sick, and I don't know if it's because I can't sleep or simply because I can't find a reason to live anymore.

I deceive myself. I lie to myself. I bump my head against the walls. I argue and always repeate the same mistakes and yet have the same desire. I get lost. I find myself. I throw myself in the trash, take myself from there, and wash myself, and yet I don't feel clean.

I hate myself. I love myself. I want myself, and yet I remain forgotten in a corner like I'm being punished. I love and hate everything around me all at the same time. I break off a piece of myself and give it to every person who gets in my way.

I want to ask for the pieces back, but what's the point after they've been trampled on? I've broken off so many pieces that I am laid bare. So barren that no one sees anything in me anymore.

It's like I'm invisible.

It's like I exist, but at the same time, I don't. My husband has forgotten about me, or so I think. He no longer sees me, no longer feels me, and no longer touches me. If I don't like what I see in me, why would he like it? He always tells me that he loves me, but I don't understand his strange way of showing it.

He always tells me that he supports me, but he is still away from home. Work has become his great love, his mistress.

I have withered like a flower, and I have shriveled up, little by little, so thirsty for love. But I have always sought love from people who cannot understand it and people who cannot give it. I have searched desperately for a drop of happiness and have stumbled over a boulder of hatred. I have offered all the best parts of me, and I am left with all the things that are more demonic.

My soul screams for a drop of peace. I run through the darkness, and I can't see the saving light. I always get lost on the paths with thorns, and no one comes to save me.

My legs are bleeding, my eyes are bleeding, and my heart is already black. I have nothing to offer and still nothing to receive. I exist only because I have to, not because I want to.

My name is Melissa, and I live in a hip neighborhood in Manhattan. I married Miguel ten years ago. Back then, he was at the police academy, and I...

I had no purpose in life.

I was lost, and my soul was tainted with all the wickedness in the world. I ran from bed to bed to hide my bleeding wounds. I don't even remember how I got into that situation.

I never knew my birth parents.

I stayed in an orphanage until the age of five when a wealthy couple adopted me. They loved me like their own child and made sure I had everything I needed. They were unable to have children, and after several failed attempts, they decided to adopt one.

I don't know if I was lucky enough to be a part of their lives or if I was just their tormentor. It couldn't be otherwise seeing that my adoptive father ran America's largest marketing company.

They both died in a plane crash when I was twenty. I had been supposed to go with them on that vacation. It should have been a family vacation, but I was too busy living a life that didn't seem to be mine as I bedded countless strangers.

Sex was like a drug to me.

I hid behind the hot bodies of the men and women I was with night after night. I didn't know how to live and face a life where I didn't feel I belonged. I didn't know how else to spend my nights so I wouldn't sleep and fall prey to the demons. I have never understood if those demons existed only in my mind or if they were part of reality, too.

I was left with all my adoptive parents' wealth under the guidance of the my adoptive father's right hand. Marc was around forty when he tried to teach me the business. I had sex with him every time we met.

He called me to the office one day. I hadn't had sex in a few days and had become somewhat agitated. I put on a white dress, quite transparent and very short. Underneath, I wore only a garter belt, no underwear or bra.

I had round and succulent breasts. When I masturbated, I caressed and kissed them until exhaustion. Today, my nipples peeked out triumphantly through the sheer material.

When I got to the office, Marc was sitting in his chair facing the window. I entered without knocking and sat down in the empty chair at his desk.

The smell of my perfume made him turn toward me. He smiled and his eyes fell on my breasts. My erect nipples let him know I was very horny. He knew this, and yet he waited every time for me to make the first move.

I was fairly sure he'd already forgotten why he'd called me to his office. He just stared at me without saying anything. His eyes did all the talking for him. I read his burning desire to penetrate me. I spread my legs and layed out everything in plain sight. He couldn't see because of the desk, but he already knew what was waiting there.

He rose from his chair and walked over to me, not even bothering to close the blind that separated his office from his secretary's. I think it excited him to the fullest to know that he was being watched. The only one that remained in the twenty-five-story building was his secretary, who always left last.

All the other employees had left two hours ago. We were on the sixteenth floor, and from the window of the office, we could see a beautiful sunset. His secretary nodded at the documents on her desk, trying not to look at us.

Marc sat on the edge of the desk and touched my left nipple.

I moaned at his touch and arched my body.

I lift the material of the dress to my waist and stroked my clitoris while putting a finger in my mouth and sucking it sensually.

No longer comfortable, Marc moved my legs apart even further then knelt in front of me and started licking my clitoris.

His hot mouth drove me crazy as his tongue pressed against my clit and brought me closer and closer to orgasm. I turned my head to the side, and before I closed my eyes at the precipice of the orgasm, I saw the secretary masturbating. That made me climax with the strongest orgasm in a while.

As Marc unbuckled his trouser belt and freed himself from the garment, I motioned for the secretary to come to us. She didn't turn down my invitation and came willingly.

While Marc pushed into me from behind, I played with her clit to bring her to orgasm. We changed positions and partners several times. It was an orgy in a real sense. After two hours, we fell on the floor, exhausted. It had been one of the most memorable sex parties ever.

When I left, Marc told me that he would take care of the problem about which he had called me to his office to discuss. It always happened that way, and I never managed to learn anything about the business.

> I wasn't even interested.

If Marc hadn't been there to take care of everything, I probably would have sold the business. I didn't care about it, and I didn't have time for business. I just liked to party every day and spend the company's money.

Alcohol and drugs were never absent from my life. I didn't even know all the people who came to my parties, but I had sex with almost everyone. New people came every time, which gave me the satisfaction of having sex with as many people as possible.

In this world, there is only one demon whose blood flowing in its veins has the power to turn humans into demons.
- Muzan Kibutsuji -

CHAPTER 4

On the day of my marriage to Miguel, I thought I had finally gotten rid of the demons that had haunted me my whole life. I thought I was in love and that I would be happy. I thought Miguel would kill all the monsters inside me, and I would become a normal person.

I thought love would work wonders.

I gave up for a while, even the therapy I had been going to since I started talking with the same psychologist I'd had all my life.

I've always had nightmares that seem so real that I can't tell the difference between reality and the dream. Ever since I was a child, I have been afraid to sleep at night, and I couldn't even manage with the sleeping pills they always stuffed in me. I often kept the pills hidden under my tongue, and after the nurse left the room, I'd spit them into the toilet.

I sometimes believe that the devil decided to throw me onto Earth when I was born. I think he wanted revenge on humanity and he sent me to destroy it. I been thrown from Hell and unleashed as hell on Earth.

I met Miguel at a party for my twenty-fifth birthday. Miguel was a shy young man, but quite attractive.

Not in that sexual sense.

It was probably the first time I'd seen a man and didn't try to have sex with him after the first conversation. Maybe this attracted me to him the most and made me feeling like I was in love with him. We were young, and we didn't know what the future held for us. We got married shortly after we met.

I never told him about my nightmares or that I considered myself crazy. The first six months of marriage were probably the most beautiful in my life and the quietest. I had given up my meetings with the psychologist because I felt better.

I even managed to sleep a few nights without having nightmares or panic attacks. When I did have them, I tried not to make too much noise and wake Miguel so I would not have to give him explanations.

I thought I would become a normal person and I would know the joy of living. I fooled myself like this until I realized I couldn't fight something I didn't know or understand. I couldn't fight with something I couldn't see, couldn't touch, and couldn't control. And I had no control over my life, and I don't think I ever did.

Two years after our marriage, Miguel graduated from the police academy and got a job as a detective. For the first four years, he did only office work and then started going out in the field. I was happy for him, but I couldn't be happy for myself.

Our marriage had become more and more monotonous. We had become two strangers living under the same roof. I often preferred sleeping as far away from him as possible because I could no longer stand his presence in bed.

He hadn't done anything to me. On the contrary, he was trying to save what was left of our marriage, and I knew he loved me as much as when we got married.

I was the one who could no longer control myself. I think I was wrong; I had never loved Miguel. I'd lied to myself for so many years about being a happy woman and finally having a normal life. We had even tried to have a child. Every time I got pregnant, I lost the pregnancy after two months.

All of my pregnancies ended in the second month. It was weird, and I didn't understand why it was happening to me. During the two months of pregnancy, I slept peacefully. I could even sleep without pills, and I had no nightmares. The day before I lost the pregnancy, I always had a hard time falling asleep, and then I would have the strangest nightmare, which could not be stopped in any way.

I always woke up in a strange room.

A red light suffused the room. A monster was approaching me. It was always the same monster. It felt like a female, but I didn't know how I could know such a thing. I knew absolutely nothing about monsters or demons, but I always saw them.

I saw myself crucified.

That monster or demon got closer and closer to me. Every time, in every nightmare, the demon stole my baby, tearing it from my womb and eating it. I always woke up terrified.

The moment I screamed and woke up, I knew I was losing my pregnancy. Blood started to flow from me as if those nightmares had been real, and my baby had really been taken and eaten by that demon.

Three times I tried to get pregnant. I got pregnant three times, and the same thing happened every time.

After that, I gave up.

I never told Miguel about my nightmares. Even the doctors could find no medical explanation for the miscarriages I had. But I knew what was happening. I knew, and yet I did not understand it.

I often missed the days when my body was touched by different hands, kissed by different mouths, penetrated by different penises. However, I had resisted for ten years and been with only one man. The demons that once haunted me probably had lost the war with me, and now others had come to win the battle.

I was going to defeat them, as I always did. I couldn't stand anyone taking control of me and my body anymore. I could no longer bear the thought of living in a hell created to destroy me. I was going to unleash Hell on Earth if that would help me be a normal person. I was going to destroy everything in my path to find my place in this world.

What has always made a Hell on Earth has been that man has tried to make it his Heaven.

- Friedrich Holderlin -

CHAPTER 5

Another sleepless night. I already know all the imperfections on the walls and the ceiling in the bedroom. Even the painting hung on the wall to my right has been carefully studied.

There are some red roses.

One rose has six petals, one has four petals, and the other two have five petals each. They have something golden in the middle. I was thinking about taking a closer look to see what they had glued under the paint.

Half of the background in the painting is painted gold, the other half brown—too dark brown for such beautiful flowers. I love roses, especially the blue ones. I know they're not natural and are just injected with that gorgeous color, but I still love them. Even so, my favorite flower remains the orchid.

The bedroom ceiling has waves.

It is clear that he was not a craftsman, the man who built this house. There is a brown spot next to the air conditioner on the wall to my left. After they did the installation, they didn't even bother applying a little white paint to cover that miserable color. I think I should call someone from the company to give this bedroom a makeover.

I can't stand looking at every imperfection every night. It is as if the weaknesses in my life are reflected in these imperfect walls. It's like remembering the scars of my life. The other bedrooms are perfect, and that's why I don't like sleeping in them.

Oddly, I prefer imperfection because that's how I feel. I feel colorless, devoid of feelings, and vacant of a zest for life. I think that I live only when I manage to fall asleep, when my mind visualizes the most horrible deeds that someone normal could ever do. Only then do I feel in control of the situation, and what I do; then I feel strong and invincible.

Sometimes I want those nightmares to be real, but at the same time, I'm terrified by the possibility that I could unleash so many demons. Demons that would take me over and the world I live in, monsters that would probably turn this world into Hell.

I plan to go for a run at night, but as if a witch has cursed me, I can't get out of the house. I've tried many times to get out of the house at night, but I can't even get to the door. Every time I walk to the door, something pulls me back. Something tells me that I don't have to go out. Something tells me that the darkness of the night will swallow me, and I will never be able to see the light of day again.

My soul is as black as night.

Dirty blood flows through my veins, and it would only spread hatred and violence if it broke out of me. Sometimes I think I have a guardian angel who tries to warn me when I'm in danger, but he doesn't always succeed because the demons drive him away.

Demons are more potent than the angel who wants to save me. I can't leave the house, and I can't sleep. I can't even have friends anymore. I'm afraid I'll do them harm.

I am afraid that the demons will take possession of them as well. I don't even know when I became so alone or when my friends disappeared from my life. I don't remember if I removed them or if they disappeared voluntarily. All I know is that I've been too busy fighting demons who want to take me over.

I will not allow them.

I will not lose the fight.

I'm sure I'll win in the end.

There must be something good in me that overcomes the evil that has taken over. I need to have a purpose in this world to stay in it as long as possible, and I hope that my last deed in this world will be a good one, worthy of being remembered by those who knew me.

I'm afraid to sleep at night.

I think I've always been afraid to sleep at night. Sometimes I probably had more courage to sleep, but other times, I was too weak to face what awaited me beyond real life. I have always felt present in several worlds at the same time.

Sleeping pills no longer work, and sometimes they cause me hallucinations. During the day, I plan to go out on the beach or wherever I can to see something other than this house that I can't stand anymore. I feel like a prisoner in my own home and in my own life.

I feel there is another person who, little by little, tries to take my place and turn me into a monster. My adoptive parents left me a letter briefly telling me the story of my childhood before I came to their house. At the orphanage where I lived for five years, three nurses performed black magic.

They used very young children so they wouldn't remember it when they grew up. They reported many cases of disappearing children up to two years of age, and many cases of death were reported of children over ten. They all seemed to be death by natural causes, so no one was ever interested in investigating those cases, and the files were closed shortly afterward.

My adoptive parents told me they'd heard rumors that I had been part of their experiments. I had escaped alive only because they'd adopted me.

So I had a sign on my back, but I was never interested in finding out what it meant. They were just rumors, and I didn't believe them. Although it was the only way to explain why I was afraid to sleep at night and couldn't be a normal person, that couldn't be right.

I felt I was not part of this world, but I was always busy trying to do what ordinary people did. I didn't know if I was a normal person or why wanted to be a normal person.

I didn't know anything about my birth parents; they had probably abandoned me because they'd felt I was a monster from the day I was born. I do not condemn them because they abandoned me, and I do not want to know about their existence.

I want to be a normal person.

I still don't know what that means because I've never been a normal person, but I'd like to know.

You cannot defeat darkness by running from it, nor can you conquer your inner demons by hiding them from the world. In order to defeat the darkness, you must bring it into the light.
- Seth Adam Smith -

CHAPTER 6

I can hardly keep my eyes open tonight. I haven't taken sleeping pills yet and I still feel like I'm going to fall into a deep sleep.

I go to the bathroom to wash my face, and I feel my legs soften. I lie down on the bed so as not to faint, and I suddenly wake up in a room that seems familiar to me. It feels as if I've been there as often as I've been home.

I'm walking down a long, very dark hallway. The moon casts its rays through the windows on the left of the hall. I follow the rays so I can walk without stumbling and falling. Now my legs are working very well, no more shaking.

I feel weird and inexplicably relieved.

It's like flying instead of walking.

The hall is very long, and, apart from the windows through which the moon shines, I see nothing else. I don't see any doors. I go forward, pushed as if by a strange force. I let myself be guided by the peculiar power until I reach a black door with strange red marks on it.

I open it quickly and feel anger and fear. My hand is shaking more and more. With an unleashed force, I slam the door. In the middle of the room is a small bed where a woman sleeps peacefully. She didn't hear the noise I made when I slammed the door.

A powerful force tells me I have to kill her.

I don't know who she is, but I enjoy the thought of killing her. I hate her, but I don't know why. I just know I want to kill her.

She sleeps.

I want to stab her with a knife forty centimeters long and three centimeters wide. I look around the room and see nothing I could use to kill her.

I feel like I have something in my right hand, and I raise my hand to look. There is a knife in my hand, and I don't understand where it came from. When I entered the room, I had nothing in my hand.

I approach the bed and think to plunge the knife into the woman's abdomen, but that seems too simple. I think I'd rather cut her throat, but that's too quick. If I cut her neck, she would die too soon. I stab her in the abdomen.

She starts screaming.

I put my hand over her mouth because I don't want her to make a fuss. I can't stand to hear screams, and I don't want to give her a chance to say anything. I want to feel good, and that makes me feel good. I twist the knife in her abdomen and take it out.

Where else can I put it?

I have to make her suffer a while before she dies. Or maybe I won't even kill her. I'll leave her like this until all her blood flows out so she'll die in agony. I stab the knife into her right thigh. She doesn't bleed too much from there, and that doesn't give me any satisfaction.

I want more blood.

I can't hold my hand to her mouth anymore, so I cover her face with a pillow, but not before I stab her in the throat. It will be deadly. A lot of blood is flowing now, and that gives me crazy pleasure. I don't know how I got into this building. I don't even know where I am.

All I know is that I want to torture her a long time before I kill her. I have to cut her more to let the blood flow from everywhere. She has such beautiful blood, a rich red color. I think she's young or maybe she's just not suffering from any disease.

The blood smells good.

I want more blood, so I start to cut her hands. I have to cut her veins. Blood flows very fast from there. I can't hear her anymore. She may have fainted. I can feel her pulse. It's very weak, but it's okay.

She's still alive.

I play with her a little more, and then I leave. Before I go, I make sure there is no life in her.

I wake up in my bed. I don't know how, but I'm lying in my bed, covering myself with the sheet and looking up at the ceiling.

I still can't sleep.

I feel a presence in my bedroom. I look around and notice that I am alone. Miguel is still working or has come home and is sleeping in another bedroom. The nights we sleep together have become rare. He works a lot at night, and, when he comes home, I barely see him. He greets me and kisses me on the forehead and then goes to his office.

I don't know what he's doing in there because I never bother him. I don't even know if he works at night or if he talks to other women. I don't blame him, and I don't have a reason to. I can't be a wife anymore; I don't think I've ever been one.

I would probably feel better if he told me he didn't love me and said he wanted to leave me. I could take that step. But, in a way, I feel better knowing that someone still lives in this house. Even though we have become two strangers and we rarely see each other, I still feel his presence in the house every day. Maybe if I had managed to have a child, he would have stayed at home longer.

Or maybe not.

I always ask myself so many questions, and I don't even bother to look for the answers. It's four in the morning, and I had another nightmare.

I didn't kill anyone; it was just my sick imagination. Or maybe I killed a woman? It seemed so real to me, and yet I don't have a knife in my hand. I don't even have bloodstains on me. I have remorse, but I don't know why.

I feel like I did a good deed.

I feel that because I killed that woman, many more human beings will survive. I try to figure out why the room seemed familiar to me, but I don't remember anything.

Maybe it was something from childhood. Over the years, I have tried to erase from my mind all the horrible memories of that time. Now I can barely remember anything from then.

I think I should sleep.

It's already morning, and my eyes are closing.

*We are all in the same game, just different levels.
Dealing with the same Hell, just different devils.*

- Jadakiss -

CHAPTER 7

I wake up from a horrible nightmare and rub my eyes. My head hurts, and I go to the bathroom to wash my face. I look in the mirror and see several demons struggling to get out of me. I fall back in fright and shake my head to return to reality.

I get up in terrible pain. I hit the tub when I fell, and my back hurts a lot. I straighten up and continue to wash my face. Everything around me seems to be spinning. I smell a weird odor. I don't understand what it is. I look at the water in my hands.

It has a strange color.

I don't know if everything that is happening now is real or if I am a prisoner in another nightmare. I look in the mirror again with fear. I see the same image of the demons coming out of me. I don't even know how many there are. I hear terrible sounds all around me. I feel like I'm going to lose control of my body. It's hard for me to fight so many demons.

My dark soul wants to give up.

It cannot bear so much pain and uncertainty anymore. I break the mirror and look for antihallucination pills in the drawer. It's the first time I've seen demons remaining in me for so long. So far, I have only felt them, and I have always tried to resist. I've held them somewhat in me without letting them come to the surface.

I am afraid for my life and the lives of those around me. I don't know if I should run and hide or sit and fight what is coming. The nightmares seem so real that I am terrified I'm capable of horrible crimes.

I'm unhappy, and I know that.

I'm unhappy, and there's nothing I can do about it. I don't have the life I want, yet I don't dare break away from it. I don't know what's going on with me, yet I don't dare find out.

My therapist always says I am like this because of the traumas I suffered as a child, but I feel entirely different. Something much darker takes me over more and more every day, something pushes me to deeds incompatible with life.

Nobody believes me.

My husband thinks I'm crazy and avoids me more and more. He is often away from home, and I feel so lonely. I struggle alone with something only I see. He has tried several times to persuade me to go to a clinic to heal. I know and feel that there is no cure for me. I feel that this time the demons will win the battle.

Or maybe I'm a demon myself?

Sometimes I feel that the real me is the person in my dreams who likes to kill and not the one who tries to have an everyday life beyond the horrible nightmares. Sometimes I get the impression that my only reality is when I fall asleep. In those nightmares, I feel strong and invincible. In those nightmares, I am not afraid of demons, and no devil takes control of me.

I have the impression that the demons kneel in front of me in those nightmares, and they will do what I command them to do. I don't know who I like more—my nightmare version of me or my real-life version of me.

I, the real one, am a sad person.

I haven't done anything special in this life, and I don't have the energy to survive. Until I married Miguel, I lived a depraved life with alcohol, drugs, and sex. That's the only way I felt alive. That's the only way I could deal with the nightmares that drove me crazy.

That's the only way I could stand every moment that I felt like I was changing. Every moment that I felt like an invisible force was watching me. Every moment that I heard my name without anyone around me.

I am a person without dreams and hopes. I don't believe in God, yet I tend to believe that there is something evil. But how could there be something evil without something divine, something right? There can't be only good or only evil; there must be both to balance the world. And yet, why don't I see the right side?

Why don't I see angels around me?

Why don't I have good feelings, and why don't I want to do good deeds? Why did only evil dominate me? Why don't angels fight demons to save me?

I ask myself all these questions as I go downstairs to make myself coffee. I'm not particularly eager to eat in the morning, so I prefer to drink only strong coffee.

Coffee and cigarettes are my only vices now. I haven't touched alcohol since the day I married Miguel. I didn't want my husband to have a wrong opinion of me from the beginning of our marriage. When I drank alcohol, I was a completely different person. I spoke vulgarly and did all sorts of nasty things.

One evening, when I'd left one club to go to another because the atmosphere had grown too monotonous, I knock down an older adult in the street.

He fell on the asphalt, and when other passersby picked him up, his face was full of blood. I started laughing when I saw the blood on his face, and I felt incredible satisfaction. Then I took my high heels off my feet and started throwing them at the passersby. The heel of a shoe stuck in a woman's head. I laughed so hard that my laughter turned strange and creepy.

One of the club's bodyguards called the police and an ambulance. I was still laughing when people started coming outside and began looking at me with fear. I don't know what they saw, but I know I wanted to do more harm.

I didn't have time though because the police came and arrested me. They locked me in a dark cell for three days. I was lucky I was a millionaire and had the best lawyers in town. Otherwise, I would have been locked up for a few years.

All of this happened shortly after my adoptive parents died. I think if they had still been alive at that time, they would have disinherited me, and they probably would have been ashamed of how depraved I had become.

*Bad people don't go to Hell,
they are already there.
- Dan Millman -*

CHAPTER 8

A new day, a new challenge to succeed at staying alive. I've been thinking a lot lately about ending my days. I feel like I'm going to do terrible things, and I don't want to hurt anyone.

I call my friend Clara to meet for breakfast. We have known each other since childhood, more precisely since I was adopted. We went to the same school, and, because I was always shy and weird, Clara tried to approach me and did not give up until she convinced me to become her friend.

We've been together ever since.

She was the only person who I could tell about issues without her ever telling me I was crazy. I don't know if she believed everything I told her, but she never tried to tell me what I should do. She was with me, and that was all that mattered to me.

I haven't seen her in a few weeks, and I know she would listen to me and understand what I want to say to her. We go to our favorite restaurant next to my inherited company. She listens to me without interruptions and then tells me it may be best to start looking for my biological parents. It might be the only way to determine what is happening to me and why I cannot be a normal person.

Clara never usually gives me advice on how to live my life, but death seems to be everywhere and primarily in the places I walk. I feel like I leave death behind me wherever my feet go. I can feel the demons lying inside me, stretching out their hands to try to kill every person around me. To kidnap their pure souls and turn them into demonic ones.

I want to walk back home. Even though it's far, I prefer to get a little movement in. I'm in no hurry to get home, and I don't want to be alone in that house anymore.

Today I want to feel the air on my skin. I want to smell the grass. I want to feel the smell of the trees. I want to enjoy every scent that comes out of restaurants and cafes. I want to enjoy every man who passes by me.

I have never done this before.

I've never walked so much. It's new, so unique as if I am seeing the world for the first time or maybe the last time. The tall buildings give me the impression that life can exist for me as well. They give me the feeling that there can be life beyond death.

The parks full of trees, flowers, and people give me a strange feeling. Some people seem real; others seem to come from another world. I stroll and admire everything around me. I get home two hours later, and my legs ache terribly. I lay down on the couch to rest. The day is almost over, and evening is coming.

The sun had set, and the reddish light came in through the windows and enveloped the room. It almost seemed romantic.

I stared at the ceiling. I was exhausted, but I tried to keep my eyes open so I would not fall asleep. After a few minutes, I got up from the couch.

Everything was weird in the house. Nothing seemed to be the way it was when I got home. It was as if I was in another place, a simple and dirty home. It smelled dreadful. There was the pungent smell of rotten food and mold. I was looking around, and I didn't realize where I was.

A force pushed me toward a door.

The house did not have inside stairs and it had few rooms. When I reached the door, my hand caught the doorknob. I opened it.

Inside there is a large bed and a dresser. Next to the bed was a table with several medicine bottles and a candle that illuminated the room. The walls of the room were black because of the mold.

A very old woman was sleeping on the bed. I approached her. I didn't know who she was, but I knew I had to kill her. I checked to see if she was alive. When I placed my hands on her, she woke up. She started screaming when she saw me and began a prayer.

I realized then that the demon had taken me over and I was no longer as I used to be. My body had become the demon's.

I pulled out the woman's tongue so she couldn't speak, and then I gouged out her eyes so she couldn't see. I took the candle from the table and let the hot wax drain into the vacant eyesockets.

Her scream of pain was deafening.

Part of me wanted to kill her as quickly as possible to end her suffering, but another part wanted to make her suffer as much as possible. Without even touching her, I lifted her from the bed with incredible force and dragged her up to the ceiling. I raised my hand toward her body, and with one finger, I made a circle around her chest and took out her heart.

Blood fell from the ceiling like torrential autumn rain. I raised both hands above me, bent my head back, and let the blood flow wet over my body. It was a scintilating pleasure to feel that hot blood dripping onto every part of my body.

I screamed with joy and woke up. This time I was in my house. I think it was another nightmare.

Or maybe it was real?

All the feelings I experience in those nightmares seem more real than those I have in real life. There are times when I don't know what my reality is. What is the real world, and what is the unreal one? Who is the real Melissa in this whole story? Who am I? I don't know myself anymore, and I don't recognize myself.

The gates of Hell are open night and day; smooth the descent, and easy is the way: but, to return, and view the cheerful skies; in this, the task and mighty labor lies.
- Virgil -

CHAPTER 9

I wake up very sweaty and short of breath. I try to get out of bed, and I can't. I don't know if a particular part of my body hurts or if my whole body hurts, but I know that I feel an indescribable pain in my soul.

My heart is broken, and I don't understand what's happened to me. I had a terrible nightmare. I was in a room that seemed familiar to me, but I didn't know where I was.

It was a modest house where, I noticed, a family with three children lived. I took each picture in my hand and studied them all. Two faces, the adults, seemed familiar to me, but I had no idea who they were. or why they seemed familiar.

I went upstairs. I opened the first door. That's where the parents slept. I opened the second door; a teenager was sleeping there. At the third door, my hand began to tremble when I wanted to open it.

I took a few deep breaths to find the courage to open the door. There were two small beds in the room. My legs went toward the little girl's bed. I didn't know why I had to be there or what I had to do, but I felt like I would do something terrible. The boy opened his eyes and looked at me.

I motioned for him to be quiet and put my hand on the girl's head. I turned her toward me and, with unbridled power, pulled out her eyes.

The boy was still looking at me, but he didn't make a sound. The little girl started screaming, and I had to cover her mouth. I put a pillow on her face, and with my other hand, I took the heart out of her chest.

I brought my hand as close to my face as possible to see her heart, and, at that moment, I noticed that my hand looked different.

The boy was frozen, and I could barely hear his breathing.

My hand was black, my fingers were much longer, and my nails were very long, sharp, and red. I raised my other hand, and it looked the same. Then I panicked and threw the girl's heart on the floor. I left the room and started running to get out of the house as quickly as possible.

As I passed the kitchen, I saw my face in a mirror near the front door. I panicked and could barely breathe in fear. I could see a head smaller than mine in the mirror, hairless, with red eyes and a deformed face. The mouth was small, and several long tongues came out of it. From the end of each tongue dripped red venom.

My body did not look like a human body.

It had different shapes.

I screamed in fear.

At that moment I woke up in my bed, and I was no longer able to move. I felt like everything was real. I wanted to go to the mirror to see if it was me or the dream monster.

In an attempt to get out of bed, I fell. My legs were shaking, and I could barely feel my hands.

I gathered all the strength I could at that moment and struggled to get up from the carpet by the bed. The mirror in my bathroom was broken, so I had to leave the room and walk down the hall to the guest bathroom. I held onto the walls with my hands, and I could barely walk. It was utterly dark, but I could still see.

When I put my hand on the doorknob in the bathroom, it started to shake. I was afraid I would see in the mirror the monster from my dream. I was fearful that I had become a monster or that the monsters in me had taken over my body before I had had the chance to find out what was happening to me.

I was glad my husband was not home. He had been sent to California for a month and would not be home for the next three days.

I opened the bathroom door and headed straight for the mirror. I closed my eyes for a few moments before looking in the reflective surface.

Afraid of what I would see, I didn't know if I was ready to be a monster. I took a few deep breaths and then opened my eyes. In the mirror, I saw myself as I was last night before I fell asleep. There was no sign of the monster from my dream.

I was relieved.

I washed my face and then went down to the kitchen to make a strong cup of coffee. I needed it to recover.

After making my coffee, I went out onto the back terrace and lit a cigarette. My lungs didn't receive the first draw of cigarette smoke very well, and I started coughing. I took a few deep breaths to recover and took another draw.

I closed my eyes to enjoy the cigarette smoke along with the taste of coffee. At that moment, an image appeared to me of my hand holding the girl's heart. I opened my eyes and began to cry.

It couldn't be true.

I wasn't able to commit such a crime.

It was still night. I could feel the cold autumn air on my skin. The trees behind the house moved quickly. The rustling of leaves seemed to turn into a song. There was a full moon. The shade from the trees appeared to come to life. Each tree had a different shape. They seemed to be dancing.

It was a great show.

I was starting to feel better. I tried to enjoy the shapes and sounds of nature. When the cold air reached my bones, I decided to go into the house for a blanket to wrap around me.

I didn't want to sleep anymore, and I would stay on the terrace until morning. When I got up from the armchair, I thought I saw a strange shadow. I stood still and looked intently through the trees.

I wasn't sure if I thought I'd seen a shadow or had even seen it at all. When I decided to go back into the house, that strange shadow appeared in front of me. Flooded with fear and dread, I could no longer move.

That shadow was a demon.

A new demon this time.

I had never seen this demon in my nightmares before. I think I fainted at that moment because when I opened my eyes, I was lying on the floor and the monster was no longer there. Had this been another nightmare, or had it been real? Had I started seeing demons in real life, or had I started sleeping with my eyes open?

I didn't understand anything anymore. I felt nothing but anger and fear. I was angry with myself because I didn't dare to discover the truth about my childhood and mad with the demons who would not give me peace. If they were going to destroy me, why didn't they? If they were going to take me out of this world, why didn't they take me?

Why did they torment and ensnare me so much?

Remember that time you let us out of the box

it was your fault

you decided to stop fighting us

you let me out.

you're lucky you're still alive

it's only a matter of time

before we're Free again.

we always win.

- Simon J Brown -

CHAPTER 10

I decided to go to a witch. I searched the internet for the addresses of all the witches that claimed to exist. I was hoping that at least one of them would help me understand what was happening to me. I'd visited several "witches" in several days. None of them wanted to talk to me or help me.

In all cases, I couldn't even say a word because I was kicked out immediately. Some said that I had many demons around me, and they couldn't help me. Others didn't say a word, but just shouted at me to go out. I was exhausted and had lost all hope.

Once I even wanted to go to church.

That had been my last choice. I didn't believe in any divine power, but I had begun to believe that demons possessed me. And if demons existed, then God must probably exist, too.

The day I decided to go to church, I had a strange feeling that something terrible was going to happen. An invisible force was telling me not to leave the house.

I made my coffee like I did every morning and went out on the terrace to enjoy the fresh air while smoking a cigarette. On the patio behind the house, I have two huge armchairs. I made myself comfortable in the red one. It's my favorite. After I finished smoking the first cigarette, I rested my head on the chair back.

I closed my eyes for a few moments to enjoy the chirping of the birds and let the Sun's rays caress my skin. The heat of the Sun made me fall asleep.

I began to hear voices telling me not to go to church. I don't know who was whispering to me because there was an intense light surrounding me, and I couldn't keep my eyes open.

When the voices got closer and started screaming at me, I woke up and jumped out of my chair, scared. When I had closed my eyes to enjoy the Sun's rays, I'd had my coffee cup in my hand, and when I jumped up scared, I spilled the coffee all over myself.

I was wearing my favorite pajamas.

I knew that I would not be able to get out the coffee stains, but I still kept the pajamas. I went into the bedroom, washed my face, and got dressed to go to church.

The voices screaming at me not to go to church made me more curious than afraid.

I decided to walk.

The church was very close to my house. When I left home, I had the feeling that someone was following me. I felt a presence behind me even though no one was there. The closer I got to the church, the more I felt afraid.

At one point, I turned to see if anyone was following me. I felt more and more intensely that someone was behind me. When I looked back, everything was dark behind me.

In front of me was day time; behind me was darkness.

I saw houses, trees, cars, and people in front of me; behind me, I saw demons reaching out to me. There were also a lot of monsters that made horrible, terrifying sounds.

I kept walking to church. Now more than ever, I had to go there.

I couldn't go back.

If I returned home, it would mean going through the darkness to the demons. It would have meant going to them voluntarily and probably staying in the dark forever.

I arrived in front of the church and climbed the first step of the few dozen that would lead me to the church door. I could barely walk up to the second step. On the third step, my body began to refuse to climb. The effort got harder and harder.

When I reached the last step, I was incredibly tired. I could barely feel my feet, and I couldn't move anymore. I wanted to move forward to enter the church, but I couldn't move.

I began to make the sign of the cross. I thought maybe that would drive the demons away from me.

It was still dark behind me. I felt a tremendous force that suddenly threw me into the dark. The demons put their horrible hands on my body, and they were pulling on me to possess me. The horrendous sounds coming from them frightened me.

I became more and more terrified.

I started screaming for help. I wasn't sure if anyone could hear me, but at least I was trying.

At last, when I opened my eyes, everything around me was white. It was light. To my right was Miguel.

He got up to approach me and calm me down. I woke up sweaty with my hands in the air, asking for help. I was shocked.

A few moments ago, I had been at church, then in Hell, and now in a hospital bed? Miguel was trying to calm me down. He told me I had been in a coma for a week.

He said I had fallen down the stairs in front of the church and gotten all the way to the street. A car had hit me and I'd hit my head. He couldn't stop the car in time.

As I listened to him, I couldn't believe such a thing was real. Apparently I could not go to church either.

Or had the demons not allowed me to enter?

It would probably still have only been a slight chance of getting rid of them even if I'd managed to get into the church. More and more, I was starting to lose hope that there was any chance I could be a normal person.

Demons do not exist any more than gods do, being only the products of the psychic activity of man.
- Sigmund Freud -

CHAPTER 11

After a lengthy search, I managed to find my birth parents. I hired a private detective and told him everything I knew about my childhood. I didn't have many details, but I hoped my money would work wonders. I told the detective to spend as much as was needed to help me.

I could no longer bear to live without knowing what is happening to me. I could no longer struggle with something I did not know and could not understand.

I found out that my parents had changed their names after they'd abandoned me at the orphanage and moved to Europe.

They had moved to a village near Sofia, Bulgaria, as far away from me as possible. My mother died shortly after she had abandoned me, and my father had lived alone in an old and creepy house. The detective managed to find a picture of my mother. I was amazed that I looked a lot like her.

She was young in the picture, probably the same age I am now. She had the same piercing black eyes, the same lost look, and the same hair color.

My father in this picture was a young, tough, strong man, but the features of the face betrayed traces of sadness and fear.

I decided to look for him to discover the truth about my life. I had to uncover the mystery behind my nightmares, and this was my only chance. Still, I had a feeling that I wouldn't like what I found out and that I would never be the same again.

I told my husband I was going on a business trip. I didn't want to tell him everything so I wouldn't scare him, too. I was terrified of everything that was happening to me enough for the both of us, particularly because I had never been able to find an explanation for my nightmares that seemed so real.

I had mixed and confusing emotions. I didn't know how my father would receive me. I hoped he could tell me about my childhood and the strange phenomena happening to me. I knew it was possible that only my mother would have known the truth, but I was hoping that they had been very close, considering that neither of them had wanted to keep me.

The flight was long and tiring. I got a room at a hotel in Sofia. I planned to rent a car the next day and look for my father.

I deposited my things in my room and went down to the bar to have a drink. I needed a lot of alcohol to be able to sleep in an unfamiliar bed in a foreign country. Nobody knew me here, so I could drink as much as I wanted without worrying that someone would recognize me.

I was also afraid that the demons had followed me here, and I was scared to be alone in the room. They had become stronger and stronger, and fear had taken over more and more.

I sat down in a high chair at the bar and ordered a glass of whiskey with ice. I wasn't going to sleep much, so I hoped the bar would be open long into the night.

At one point, I felt a hand caressing my back and a voice whispering in my ear.

"You are incredibly sexy. I want to believe you're alone tonight."

I wore a long white dress with an open back. He stroked my back with his fingertips. A finger stopped at the mark on my back, and he made a strange sign with his finger on my scar.

I didn't want to look back at him.

I closed my eyes and enjoyed the sensations that passed through my body when he touched it. I think he noticed that I liked it.

He started to kiss my neck while his hands moved slowly over my back. I hadn't felt such sensations in a long time. I hadn't felt pleasure in a few years.

Sometimes I even wondered why my husband wasn't leaving me because our relationship had become more friends than lovers.

Finally, I turned my gaze to him and invited him to sit next to me.

I was amazed by his beauty and charm.

He was a very tall and exquisite man. I was sure that under those business clothes, his body deserved to be touched and kissed. His muscles seemed to want to burst from the material of his suit. He looked more like a wrestler than a man sitting in a chair at an office all day.

I had started my third glass when we decided to get acquainted. I found out that his name was

Kalmin and that he was here to close an important business deal.

I didn't dare tell him why I had come here, so I changed the subject whenever he tried to find out more about me. I wasn't going to tell a stranger about my life.

He seemed to be a man who only wanted sex from a woman, and yet he talked more than I did. I lost track of the number of glasses of whiskey I drank. I apologized to Kalmin and went to my room to sleep for a few hours so I wasn't drunk on my first meeting with my father.

I didn't wait for him to say anything because I quickly ran away so fast that I almost fell. I could barely stand, and I could scarcely see the elevator door.

I managed to get into the elevator without stumbling a second time, and I pressed the button for the seventh floor. As the doors began to close, I saw a hand trying to stop them.

It was Kalmin.

It seemed I wasn't as fast as I had hoped and hadn't managed to run away from Kalmin. I knew I would not be able to resist the temptation to tear off his suit and have sex with him.

He seemed to have the same thoughts as I did. He entered the elevator. While we made the ascent, he pressed the emergency button to stop the elevator.

He pushed me up against the cold mirror. I shuddered at the cold feeling on my body. A strange sound escaped from me as he pressed against me and I felt something hard.

With his right hand, he grabbed my hair. With his left hand, he stroked my hips. I could feel his hands lifting up my dress, revealing my long legs.

Suddenly he assaulted me with kisses, leaving me breathless. It was the first time I had felt so good. It was the first time I had felt every inch of my skin tremble at the touch of a man. Incredible sensations passed through my whole body, but especially in that special area.

hen his fingers pushed aside the material of my panties, I lost my breath for a few seconds. Just a few moments of tenderness and caressing were enough to give me the strongest orgasm I'd ever had.

The elevator started up again toward the seventh floor, and I wanted more and more pleasure. When the doors opened, I took Kalmin by the hand and led him to my room. I didn't care anymore that I was married. I no longer cared about my husband's love or the fact that I had been faithful for ten years.

All I wanted now was to have sex, as much wild sex as possible, to recover the ten years lost with one man. That one man had become so selfish lately that he thought only of his pleasure. He had a bizarre way of loving me, and I had never been able to understand him, probably because I was too busy fighting the demons inside me.

Tonight I was not going to let any demons destroy my pleasure. I liked Kalmin, and I liked the feelings he gave me with every touch.

I was right.

His body had only muscles that bulged firmly against his taut skin. I had never seen a man so strong and also so romantic. His freshly shaven face inspired fear, but his blue eyes said he needed love. The combination just drove me crazy.

I think I was starting to fall in love with him. I think I was beginning to want to see him in my bed every day. The tattoos on his arms made him even sexier and more attractive. His movements while having sex drove me crazy. It was as if he had always known me and knew how to give me the ultimate pleasure.

I hadn't even known I had so many parts of my body where I could get aroused. The sex that night was not as wild as I would have liked, but it was much more than I could have ever imagined I could get from a man.

I asked him to sleep with me that night.

We were lying in bed, still naked and sweating, and I reached out for him. He hugged me with his long, strong arms. I needed that hug. I felt protected and calm in those arms. I felt like this was all I needed to be happy. I fell asleep happy with a smile on my face.

I love good and pleasure,

I hate evil and pain,

I want to be happy, and I am not mistaken in believing,

that people, angels, and demons

have those same inclinations.

- Nicolas Malebranche -

CHAPTER 12

The rays of the Sun shining through the curtains caressed my face. I woke up. I was in a room full of children. I was a child, too. There were many beds in the room, and children screaming or crying.

An older woman dressed in a long black dress opened the door and began to scream. All the children became silent and froze. She was old; her skin was wrinkled and her eyes were so black that I froze in fear. She told us in an authoritative tone that we must go to eat.

The children began to walk out of the door one by one. I was the last one. When I tried to go out, the woman stopped me. She grabbed my hand and squeezed it so hard it hurt. I started to cry in pain, and she pulled me after her down a long, dark hallway.

I didn't know where I was.

At the end of the hall stairs led to a black door with a large red sign. I couldn't see the sign because of the tears flowing from my eyes. I was feeling more and more afraid. I didn't understand what she was going to do to me nor did she seem to care that I could barely breathe through my sobs.

She opened that dark door and threw me into a room. She turned and left, locking the door behind her. A red light and many candles lit the room. Two women were in the room.

They were wearing long red dresses.

They had masks covering their faces.

I could only see their eyes.

I saw two beds without mattresses. On one bed was a child bound with chains and had something in his mouth that I couldn't figure out.

The women grabbed my arms and put me on the other bed, also tying me with chains. I started to cry even harder, demanding and calling for help. I likely had no chance of being heard by anyone who cared.

They started muttering something in a language I didn't know. I had never heard such speech before. I grew even more afraid.

One of the women approached the other child's bed. I think he was a boy—I couldn't see him very well—and the other woman approached my bed.

They placed us face-to-face, me with the other child. The woman next to the other bed took out a strange object from the boy's mouth. Between us was a black bowl with a red mark out of which came black smoke.

They held us with our faces toward the bowl between us and started muttering something again.

I saw that black smoke begin to move.

I froze in fear.

Soon the smoke split in two. One side came toward me, and the other side went toward the other child. The women began to sing something in that same strange language when a red shadow suddenly emerged from the black smoke.

The two women stopped chanting and knelt. The red shadow went toward the other child, and I started screaming. The shadow stood over the child and began to take on the shape of a monster. I screamed as loud as I could, thinking that maybe I would be able to stop the madness or perhaps someone would hear me and come to save us.

I saw the red monster turn its face toward me. Before making any more sound, it appeared above me. I froze and remained motionless. The other child made no sound, and I didn't understand how he could be so calm. The red monster put a finger to my lips and started to smell me.

The women began muttering something again in that language I didn't know, and the red monster turned into a shadow again and entered me. I screamed so loud and woke up.

This time I woke up in the hotel room. Kalmin took me in his arms and tried to calm me down.

I was crying and trembling with fear.

His presence there next to me made me calm down faster than I would ever have managed on my own. This man had something in him that made me feel protected. He had an energy that helped me feel peace around me.

I wished he would never let me out of his arms. I had never felt so protected.

But as much as I liked being there with him, I remembered why I had come here. I quickly got dressed and went down with Kalmin to the hotel reception. I asked the front desk to call me a taxi.

I didn't feel able to get there on my own.

Kalmin said he would have liked to go with me, but unfortunately he had a meeting in the hotel's conference room, and he was already late.

We said goodbye, and I left to meet my father. He wasn't expecting my visit. I wanted to see his reaction and see if he would recognize me.

The child inside me has lost its way in the woods and running all around, crying and screaming.

Every time I close my eyes, I see him staring back at me and running towards me until someone wakes me back up.

And here I am, just hoping he doesn't get caught by my demons.

- Akshay Vasu -

CHAPTER 13

An hour later, I arrived at the address the detective had given me for my parents. The entire ride, I had been thinking about the latest nightmare I had. I couldn't tell if it was just a nightmare, or if it was a real memory from when I was a kid. More than ever, I needed to know the truth about my childhood. There were too many mysteries I found difficult to decipher, and that terrified me more and more.

When the driver stopped in front of a house that was almost in ruins, I was shocked. I asked him if he had the wrong address, and he assured me that it was correct. I don't know why, but I started crying.

I should not have felt any pity for my father or for the situation in which he lived because he and my mother had not felt any remorse when they had abandoned me. I got out of the taxi and sat for a few minutes just looking at the house where my father was living.

It was small and incredibly old.

The walls of the house were crooked and beginning to crack. Instead of glass windows, it had plastic coverings flapping in the wind. The roof was full of holes. The front door didn't look like the door that it was supposed to be; it consisted of several planks placed in a strange configuration.

I looked around and noticed that the rest of the houses were regular and well maintained. Only this place seemed like it had been abandoned and uninhabited by humans. I could not understand how someone could survive in this house, mostly because it was freezing outside.

It was winter.

Smoke came out of all the others homes from chimneys on the roofs, but nothing came out of this one.

I headed for what appeared to be the front door before I could change my mind and leave. I knocked on the door and heard a lost voice telling me to enter. It was dark in the house, but I noticed a lit candle by a bed.

On the bed sat an older man with white hair and a sad face. His gaze was vacant. He was not looking at me, but he knew I was there. I approached him slightly. His gaze remained as lost as before.

He told me to sit down. Did he know who I was? Did he not even look at me and knew who I was?

"I was waiting for you. I knew you would come in the end."

"Do you know me? I asked him in fright. His gaze was as lost as when I entered the house. That's when I realized he might be blind.

"You're my daughter who I abandoned thirty years ago. I'm blind, but I can feel you. You are blood from my blood."

I started to feel more and more pity for him. He lived in inhuman conditions; he was blind, and yet he recognized me. How was that possible?

"I guess you've finally decided to find out why I abandoned you. I wish this had never happened, but it was something your mother and I couldn't control."

"Before entering this house, I only felt hatred for you. I never understood why you left me. I never looked for you because I didn't want to see two people who could give up their child."

"And now you came here because something strange is happening to you and you need explanations?"

"How do you know?"

"If you came here to find out the truth, it means that you are ready for what I will tell you. Do you have nightmares at night? Are nightmares so real you feel like you've killed someone? Do you have the feeling that there are forces inside you that you cannot control?"

"Yes," I told him in amazement because he knew so much about me even though he had abandoned me when I was a child.

"What I'm going to say to you now will seem like part of a book or a movie, but I assure you it's the truth. I don't have long to live anymore, and I'm glad you decided to come before I die. If I died before you came, you would never have known the truth."

I was beginning to tremble with fear. It felt like the same fear from the nightmare of the night before.

"Before I met your mother, I was married to another woman. We had been married for a while, but our marriage didn't work out after I met your mother. I divorced her shortly after realizing I loved your mother."

"My ex-wife didn't accept it easily. She became so insistent that she came to our house. I had moved into the house where your mother lived. She came even at night. She followed your mother everywhere and always threatened her. She had become obsessed.

"That's when we decided to sell the house and move. She had just found out that your mother was pregnant, and I had to protect her. I was afraid that my ex-wife would do something bad to your mother now that she was pregnant. She and I had had no children. She couldn't have any, and that's part of why our marriage ended.

"We managed to sell the house and move as far away from her as possible. The day we left, my ex-wife came to us and started cursing your mother who was six months pregnant. She started to say something in a strange language and made some strange signs over your mother's pregnant belly.

"I didn't realize what she had done to your mother until the night she started having nightmares. In those dreams, she saw a strange monster coming to take her child.

"We decided to go to a witch. The first one refused us from the moment we entered her door. She told us that a demon was following us and she couldn't help us with anything. That's when I knew we had to look for stronger witchcraft.

"I found a new witch a few days before you were born, but it was too late. She told us that your mother was cursed by black magic far too strong to be unleashed by a single witch. She told us that the demon Abyzou was going to take you.

"Abyzou is a devil who causes abortions, who feeds on children. She told us that the demon would come and take you immediately after you were born; however, she did not understand why the demon waited for your birthday. She said that our only chance for your survival was to summon another demon who would fight Abyzou, but it was possible that that demon would haunt you for life.

"I wanted to save you. You were our first child, you were our happiness, and I couldn't give up on you. We accepted her offer without really thinking about the consequences.

"The next day, your mother went into labor, and a few hours later, you were born. We were thrilled to hold you. You had the face of an angel and a look that offered us peace.

"We were alone in the hospital room when we felt a presence near us. We were frozen in fear. You started crying. You were crying so hard, and I didn't know what to do to calm you down. It got dark in the room, and we started hearing some terrible sounds.

"I was holding you tightly, and we were both shaking with fear. Suddenly, something snatched you from my arms. You were silent; you weren't crying anymore.

"After a few moments, you started screaming again, and the light came on. You were laying on the floor without your clothes on and facing the floor. I froze when I saw the marks on your back. Your mother and I started crying and praying.

"I didn't say anything to the nurses, and we left the hospital that night. The next day, we took you to the witch who had helped us. She told us that the demon she enchanted to defend you from Abyzou had marked you. That you would be his forever. The witch told us that he would come to take you to be his bride when you turned thirty-five.

"We went home. Days of torment and nightmares followed. You were not a child like any others. While you slept, you spoke in a language we didn't know, and strange voices and sounds were always heard in your room.

"That's when we decided to take you to an orphanage. We had heard of an orphanage where spells were cast to destroy demons trying to enter children. It was so hard for us to make this decision, but we thought it was best for you.

"They told us we are not allowed to visit you for a while. When we still insisted on seeing you, a very old woman with a sinister look told us that we would never be able to see you again because the demon who had marked you was too strong. She told us that if we ever tried to look for you, we would die. Your mother and I started crying. We had broken hearts, and we had wanted so much to see you at least once more.

"Three years later, I found out you had been adopted. I didn't understand how such a thing was possible. Your mother decided to look for those who adopted you. You were our child, and we wanted you back. We did not intend to abandon you; we just wanted to do everything necessary so you could be a normal child, to have a normal life.

"Your mother found out where the family that had adopted you lived. We tried so many times to talk to them to ask them to let us see you at least once. They refused to talk to us every time.

"After two years of this, your mother decided to go to the school you were attending. She had fallen ill and wanted to see you at least once before she died.

"I don't know if she managed to see you or not because she died while she was coming home. She was waiting near the pedestrian crossing for the light to turn green so she could cross the street. A car sped through and hit the traffic light pole next to her. The traffic light fell on her head and splattered her brain on the street.

"That's when we realized that the woman at the orphanage had indeed cursed us. I went blind shortly after your mother died. Since then, I have lived with the same desire, to have the opportunity to tell you the truth before I died. To tell you that we did not abandon you and that you should not hate us anymore. I have suffered every day, and every day I wanted to be in your mother's place."

A witch ought never be frightened in the darkest forest...

Because she should be sure in her soul that the most terrifying thing in the forest was her.

- Terry Pratchett -

CHAPTER 14

I was crying and trembling. I felt a huge pain and couldn't believe I was just some diabolical plan. However, I now understood why those strange things were happening to me and why I had those terrible nightmares.

I still needed time to understand and process everything I had heard. My father motioned for me to sit next to him. I got up from my chair and, with fear, sat down next to him. He put his hand on my face and began to study it with his fingers.

"You are beautiful, much more beautiful than I would have imagined," he said with tears in his eyes.

I could see so much pain and sadness in his eyes that I started to cry and hugged him. It was so cold in that little house that I was frozen and could barely feel my hands.

He was so weak.

I could almsot see his bones. He was still my father, the one to whom I owed something because I was alive today.

I called a taxi and took him with me to the hotel. It was past midnight, and I wasn't going to leave him in this house anymore.

I had enough money to buy him the most luxurious house in Sofia and hire the best medical staff to care for him. He had suffered throughout his life. At least now, in his old age and in his last days of life, I could offer him everything he had never had. I took him with me.

In the beginning he resisted, saying that he didn't have much time to live and he didn't deserve such a gesture from me. However, he regretted that my mother had died far too young and that she was not here with us to enjoy my presence. I let him sleep in my room. I ordered room service and let him enjoy a little comfort and warmth. I went down to the front desk to get another room.

Kalmin appeared behind me while I was talking to the receptionist. I felt him long before he approached me and kissed me on the neck. He told the receptionist that it was unnecessary to prepare another room for me because I would sleep in his room.

I was amazed and smiled.

I liked the idea, and I felt the need to be with him. I hugged him and kissed him on the cheek.

I asked him to go with me to the bar. I needed a strong drink. I drank the first glass of whiskey without breathing. Kalmin was shocked.

After ordering the second glass, I started to cry. I could no longer hold in the tears and pain I felt in every cell of my body. Kalmin was shocked to see me crying and took me in his arms. He stroked my hair with indescribable tenderness.

I had never felt so much love.

This man had something indisputably reassuring about him, so reassuring that I calmed down far too quickly when I felt his strong arms around me. I think I was starting to fall in love with him.

He had appeared in my life in such a mysterious way, and almost eerily, he had the power to calm me just with a simple hug. I wanted to be able to tell him about everything that was happening to me.

I wanted to be able to tell him everything I had found out a few hours ago. I wanted so badly to be able to tell him what I was going through every day. I wanted to share with him all my pain and be able to feel like a normal woman for the first time in my life.

He lifted my head from his shoulder, took my face in his giant palms, and looked me in the eye. "I know you want to tell me something. I know you suffer, and you want to say so much, but stay calm. I have patience, and I will wait until you are ready."

I was shocked.

Was this man able to read my thoughts? Why did he care so much about me? Why was he so tender and loving with me? He had only known me for a day and he was already worrying so much about me? No one had ever treated me as nicely as he did. No one had ever paid attention to my needs, my feelings, my life.

"How do you know I want to say something? Can you somehow read thoughts? Who are you?"

"I can see how much pain your eyes hide, and I felt from the first moment I saw you that you have a brutal fight with your own life. I know you are a special woman, and I will always be with you if you will let me. I won't force you to do something you don't want to do, but I can be your shadow if you wish."

When I heard the word "shadow," I began to tremble. I remembered the red shadow in my nightmare. Was Kalmin the demon that had possessed me? Was he the shadow that had taken me over? Had he come to pick me up? But if so, why was he acting so nicely with me?

I pulled out from his arms and started running. I ran until I reached the door of my room. I didn't want to take the elevator and allow him to come after me.

At my door, I remembered that my father was there and that I had nowhere to sleep. I didn't want to bother him. I leaned against the door and slid down until I reached the floor. I put my knees to my chest and wrapped my arms around them. I started crying again.

Kalmin came up next to me.

When he sat down next to me, I began to tremble, and I looked up at him with fear. I wasn't ready to die yet. I didn't want to die.

"You don't have to be afraid of me. I don't want to harm you."

"I'm not afraid of you," I lied. "Why do you think I'm scared of you?"

I didn't want to tell him that I was afraid of him. I didn't want him to know. But maybe I was wrong, and he didn't want to hurt me. Perhaps he wasn't the demon who had taken my soul when I came into this world. Maybe I was just being paranoid, especially after everything my father had told me.

"You started shaking when I sat down next to you. I don't know why you ran away from me, and I'm sorry if I said something wrong. Please calm down. I promise I will never do you any harm."

With that, I decided to trust him. No matter how much fear and anxiety I had felt in those moments, everything suddenly disappeared as if nothing had happened when he'd approached me. I rested my head on his shoulder.

He hugged me.

I felt calm again.

I think I was starting to enjoy the peace he offered me more and more.

He took me in his arms and went toward the elevator. He pressed the button for the top floor and inserted a key at the bottom of the controls. I didn't even know where he was taking me, but the fact that I was in his arms meant everything to me.

I didn't care about anything but the incredible peace he gave me. When the elevator doors opened, we walked straight into a vast room. I think it was an apartment. It was very luxurious. I was still in Kalmin's arms. He put me down on a huge couch and returned a few minutes later with a tray full of delicious food.

Only then did I realize that I had forgotten to eat anything all day. Then he brought over a bottle of wine and two glasses.

This was the first time a man had been so careful with me. I think it was the first time I had had a romantic dinner, or so his gesture seemed to be.

He was so gentle with me, and I didn't understand why he was doing all this considering he didn't know me. He knew nothing about me, and indeed, if he found out, he would disappear from my life without a trace.

As much as possible, I would try to hide from him everything that happens to me. In any case, I would be leaving this place tomorrow, so it was unknown if we'd even ever see each other again.

After we ate, we both remained on the couch, and he just held me in his arms and stroked my hair.

"I wish I could see you again," Kalmin told me with his gentle voice.

"I leave tomorrow, and I don't know when I'll be back here. I will pay to let my father stay in this hotel for a while, and then I will decide what to do with him. I have to tell you something. I don't want to ruin our last beautiful night together, but you have to know. I am married.

"I know you're married," Kalmin said with a smile on his face.

"How do you know?"

"You have proof on your finger."

We both started laughing. I had forgotten that I was still wearing my wedding ring. "There is nothing left in my marriage anymore, and this is the first time I cheated on my husband."

"Do you regret that you did it?"

"To be honest, no. I'm not sorry because I have the right to happiness. I was too young when I got married. Even though I'm married, I feel more lonely than ever. My husband is always at work or gone because of work. We barely see each other or even exchange a few words. You make me feel something I've never felt before. You give me peace and help me calm down when I never thought I might have a chance to be calm. You have an energy that gives me peace. When I'm in your arms, I feel protected. I have never felt protected. There are many things in my life that you don't know, and, if you find out, you will probably disappear forever."

"I have patience. I'm here with you because I felt a strange but pleasant attraction from the first moment I saw you the first night at the bar. I'm here to get to know you, not to run away from you. I'm here because I feel the need to protect you. Something tells me I need to protect you."

I fell asleep in his arms, and in the morning, I woke up right there. I noticed that he hadn't even moved so he wouldn't wake me. I think it was the first time I had slept at night and hadn't had a nightmare. I think it was the first night I hadn't been afraid to sleep and the first night I had slept so peacefully.

You wake up every morning to fight the same demons that left you so tired the night before, and that, my love, is bravery.
- a.l.h. -

CHAPTER 15

My flight was at noon, so I went to my room to talk to my father as soon as I woke up. He looked so much better than when I had taken him out of that house. Now he had clean clothes, too.

I told him that he could stay in the hotel for a while and that I would hire a nurse to take care of him at all times. I was hoping he wouldn't refuse me, so I wouldn't have to convince him. To my surprise, he agreed.

I said goodbye and left. I stopped at the front desk to reserve his room for a few weeks. Kalmin was waiting for me in front of the hotel. I said goodbye to him with tears in my eyes. I wished I could stay longer.

I wished I could leave everything behind and stay with him. But first I had to understand what was happening in my life and find a solution to all my problems. If I wanted to be truly happy, I had to make sure that I was not and would not be a danger to the people around me.

As soon as I got to the airport, I wished I could go back to Kalmin. Stopped in front of the terminal, I didn't know whether to go in or go back to him. My heart told me to go back; my reason told me to go into the airport. They were both yelling at me simultaneously, and it was hard for me to make a decision.

Something pushed me into the airport.

My feet were going to the airport, and my heart was flying to Kalmin. I boarded the plane with tears in my eyes. I knew I would regret this decision. I knew it would hurt more than ever because I had given up love. Only now did I realize that I had never felt such love for my husband.

I took a book out of my bag to read. I had the seat by the window. The other two seats next to me were still vacant. I leaned my head against the window and looked outside. I just held the book in my hands. I was not ready to read it yet because I was crying. I felt someone sit in the chair next to me, but I didn't bother to look.

I was still crying.

I feel a hand cover my hand. I started to cry even harder without looking to see who was touching me. Then I felt a hand on my face, and it wiped away my tears.

I looked up next to me. It was Kalmin. I was shocked. I started to cry and leaned into his arms. This time I was crying with happiness.

"What are you doing here? You said you had to stay. Do you know that I didn't even get a chance to ask you where you live?"

"I canceled all my meetings. They can wait. I saw how sad you were when you left the hotel, and I couldn't bear to see you like that. I told you I have an incredible attraction to you that I can't control. I couldn't stay away from you. I feel like I have to be around you all the time to protect you. I live in Chicago, but I'm coming with you to Manhattan."

"I hope you haven't forgotten that I'm still married?"

We both started laughing. Now I didn't care that I was married. I was still in shock having Kalmin next to me on the plane. I was happy, though.

When we got to New York, I went with him to his hotel, and I stayed with him that night.

My husband didn't know when I was supposed to get home, and I don't think he was interested in finding out. Lately, he was away from home most of the time and always made the excuse of having a lot of work and having some significant and urgent cases he had to solve.

I had never thought of divorcing him, and I had always been to blame. I thought I had been the one who had ruined our marriage because I was always sick. I was still depressed, and many times I couldn't even get out of bed. Only now I did realize that I needed love and attention, peace, and protection.

Miguel always took his time with work. More and more work. He often worked even at night, or so he told me. He always said to me that he loved me, but he never had time to show me his love. He always assured me that there were no problems in our marriage, but his eyes were lying. He could barely touch me.

I was afraid he might have someone else, another woman, who fulfilled his carnal desires, another woman who touched his body and kissed his lips. I had been scared to ask him, fearful that maybe the answer would be yes or perhaps it would hurt me knowing he was cheating on me. He had the right to do so. I was in another world most of the time.

He didn't even bother to take me with him to the events he was invited to. He didn't ask me to go have dinner anymore. He was probably ashamed to go out in public with me.

I had become very pale.

I had lost a lot of weight.

I could not cover the circles around my eyes with make up anymore. I hadn't cared about myself anymore. I had always stayed in my pajamas around the house. When I did go out or went to the office, I'd dressed in the worst clothes, clothes that made me look more like a man than a woman. I'd always worn a hat and sunglasses.

I didn't like the person I had become either, but I couldn't do anything to improve my condition. And yet Kalmin had seen something completely different in me. He had seen beyond my clothes and appearance.

Even if I had decided to wear an elegant dress that night, it hadn't changed the fact that I didn't look like a normal woman anymore. Kalmin had seen something I couldn't see either, something I didn't think existed anymore. He had seen hope, love, and the future.

There are humans versus humans in a jungle of predators; humans full of judgment, full of blame, full of guilt, full of emotional poison—envy, anger, hate, sadness, suffering. We create all these little demons in our mind because we have learned to dream of Hell in our own life.

- Miguel Ruiz -

CHAPTER 16

The day after we arrived in Manhattan, I went home. To my amazement, Miguel was home. I had sent him a message a few hours before to let him know I would be coming home today, but I didn't expect to find him at home.

When I entered the house, he hugged and kissed me as he had never done before. It seemed strange. Had he found out that I had cheated on him? Did he know that he would lose me, and now he was trying to conquer me again? He invited me to go into town, but I refused because I was tired.

I went up to the bedroom. I wanted to take a shower and sleep. I hadn't slept all night. I had made love to Kalmin all night. We had both gotten too involved in this madness, and I was afraid it wouldn't end well.

I could still feel his hands on my body. I could still feel his lips on mine. I could still hear his voice whispering words I had never heard before.

I was distraught and didn't know how to define what I felt for him, but I knew one thing for sure. I had fallen in love with him.

When I entered the bedroom, I had a sudden feeling of anxiety. I had the impression that I would never be able to sleep in this bed again. I had the impression that the demons were waiting for me to take control of me forever. This time I felt them closer than ever. This time I felt that my end was near. I finally went into the bathroom.

I undressed and got into the shower. I noticed that Miguel had put up a new mirror, but I didn't dare look at my face in it.

After I got out of the shower, I found Miguel lying on the bed. I thought he had already gone. He got up and came to me.

He took off my towel and started stroking and kissing me. I tried to push him away, but I couldn't. It was as if I no longer had the strength to react. We were heading toward the bed when I suddenly saw my face in the mirror. I stood still for a few moments. Miguel walked away from me so he could see me.

I was terrified.

In the mirror, I saw a horrible monster.

It was the first time I had seen such a huge demon. It was the first time I had seen my affliction so clearly. My face no longer existed; my body no longer existed. I could only see a colossal demon. He had a black body and a red head, and his eyes were gold and gleaming.

His body looked human.

He had human legs and strong arms like a man, but he had no skin. I could see every red vein and every black muscle in his body. It was a strange combination. And those eyes... those golden, gleaming eyes made me shiver.

He started smiling.

I screamed in fear, and I think I fainted. When I woke up, I was already in bed. Miguel also looked terrified. He said he had seen the demon, too. For a few moments, my husband had no longer seen me, only the demon.

He looked panicked and frightened. I told him everything I knew. He couldn't believe he had lived with me for so many years and had never known what I was struggling with.

I didn't tell him about the crimes I had committed in my nightmares. I could see the regret in his eyes. I felt sorry for him, and I could see the pain in his eyes. It was too late now to do anything for me.

He stayed with me all night.

He called work and said he needed a night off. I didn't want to be alone that night. If I were left alone, I probably would not have the chance to live. I fell asleep in his arms, but I woke up at one point.

I was in a dark room.

I couldn't see anything, but I could feel someone's breath. I tried to find some way to light the room, but I couldn't find anything. Suddenly several candles lit up around me.

Otherwise the room was dark, and I didn't understand where I was. I turn to see what was behind me.

I screamed in horror.

My husband, Miguel, had been crucified on the wall. Blood flowed from his hands and feet. His head was tilted to the right. I could hear his shallow breathing, but he wasn't conscious.

An incredible force told me that I had to take out his heart and eat it. Part of me wouldn't let me do that. I started to cry and got closer to him. I raised my hand to wake him.

Tears of blood flowed from his eyes.

When he opened his eyes, they were red. I put my hand to my mouth to stop the scream that wanted to come out.

I felt a presence behind me. I turned back toward it, but I didn't see anyone. Still, I felt like someone was there with us. Someone told me I had to take his heart out of his chest and eat it.

I heard a voice in my mind repeating the same words to me. I couldn't control myself anymore. I could no longer control my body and my thirst for blood. I didn't want to hurt Miguel, but I couldn't stop what I was going to do.

I felt something push me toward Miguel. My hand went into his chest. I ripped his heart out in a split second. I held it in my hand and looked at it. Without being able to control my hand, I brought it to my mouth. All the while, I felt like someone else was controlling my body.

After I ate his heart, I started screaming.

I woke up terrified.

This time I was in my bed, and Miguel was sleeping next to me. He hadn't even heard me when I screamed. I was happy to see that my husband was still alive. It was the first time I had had a nightmare in which he also appeared. I couldn't understand why he had appeared in my nightmare.

There are moments when, even to the sober eye of Reason, the world of our sad humanity must assume the aspect of Hell.
- Edgar Allan Poe -

CHAPTER 17

I went downstairs to make my coffee. I had the same routine every morning. It had become such a habit that sometimes it drove me crazy. I was still thinking about the nightmare in which I was killing Miguel. I didn't love him anymore, but I didn't want to hurt him either.

He had been with me for so many years, and he didn't deserve the life I offered him. I grabbed my coffee and headed for the terrace door. When I passed Miguel's office, I saw that the door was open.

He never left the door open or unlocked. Lately, he had locked the office door and often stayed locked in the office at night. He always said that he had some significant and complicated cases that he is working on.

There were a lot of papers and pictures on his desk. I went in and started looking at them. The first picture I picked up made me tremble with fear. In the picture was a man who seemed familiar to me. Below that picture were several others.

One of them showed a house with a red door. I dropped the picture, and I wanted to scream. I put my hand to my mouth so I wouldn't wake Miguel. The man in the picture was the same man I had had sex with and killed in my nightmare.

I looked at the other pictures as well. All the victims in the photographs were the victims from my nightmares.

I had killed those people.

I had thought they were just nightmares.

I had thought I was just dreaming.

How was this possible?

It couldn't be true.

I was always asleep and woke up in my bed. I never had any traces of blood on me or murder weapons in my hand. I woke up precisely as I was before I fell asleep. How was it possible for me to be a murderer? How was it possible that I was the killer of these people?

And that child?

That little girl?

Why did I kill her?

Why did I kill those people?

I started crying.

Everything was getting more and more confusing. I didn't understand anything anymore. As I left the office, I heard Miguel's footsteps. I went to the terrace to drink my coffee. I felt the need to smoke and disappear from this world.

I couldn't stand the thought of killing so many people. I was shaking when Miguel came to me. He went to the living room and brought me a blanket. He thought I was shivering with cold, but I was shaking with fear.

I wiped away my tears before Miguel saw me crying. He kissed my forehead and sat down next to me.

"I saw the door to your office open, and I went inside. I saw the pictures on the desk. Are those the cases you've been working on for so many months?"

My voice trembled as I asked him. I had to behave as naturally as possible to not give him anything to suspect.

"I'm sorry you saw those scenes. I forgot to lock the door last night. Yes, those are the cases I've been working on for so long. Those are some unusual and challenging cases."

"Did you catch the criminals?"

"The killer," he corrected. "No, I didn't catch the killer. I think there's only one killer in this case. I think the killer knew those people and wanted revenge on them. There are no fingerprints or evidence to point to a suspect. The weapons with which the crimes were committed were not found either. There weren't even any signs of an break ins."

I didn't know what to say. I was afraid to say anything else so I wouldn't seem suspicious. I needed to change the subject and turn Miguel's attention to something else so he wouldn't continue telling me about those crimes.

I told him that I wanted to separate. I told him I needed time to be alone for a while. He looked at me without saying anything.

He had probably expected that, or he had probably wanted it, too. There was no point lying to ourselves anymore about having a happy marriage. There was no point in living together in the same house when we could no longer be husband and wife. I moved out a few days after that conversation.

I really didn't want to live in that house. I had too many unpleasant memories there. I wanted to start over in a new place. Maybe I would manage to have at least a few quiet days and nights.

For the first three days, I stayed at my adoptive parents' house. It was huge and very luxurious. I was not that fond of it, and I was going to sell it. It was too big for me. For now, I would let Miguel stay in it.

I wanted to buy a small and modest house or maybe an apartment.

We were divorced shortly after. I knew I was going to divorce him the day I told him we needed to separate, but I didn't dare tell him then. I didn't know what his reaction would be.

He did not refuse. He couldn't do otherwise after one evening I saw him with an exquisite and beautiful woman. They were having dinner at our favorite restaurant. I happened to pass by that night and saw them by chance. I caught them while Miguel was putting a ring on her finger.

They probably had had a relationship long before he divorced me. Maybe that's why he spent nights away from home. Perhaps she was the reason he didn't refuse when I told him I wanted to separate.

It didn't hurt me to see him happy. I was actually delighted for him. He deserved to rebuild his life and be loved. He deserved to have everything I couldn't offer him.

Tact is the ability to tell someone to go to Hell in such a way that they look forward to the trip.
- Winston Churchill -

CHAPTER 18

I met up with Kalmin several times before he left for Chicago. He had some problems to resolve, but he promised to come back as soon as possible.

In the meantime, I bought an apartment. Miguel left out house soon after the divorce. Neither of us could live in our house anymore, and I wasn't going to keep it.

My father died a few days after I returned to Manhattan. I couldn't go to Sofia, Bulgaria, to handle the necessary arrangements, but I hired someone to take care of him. He was cremated, and I would receive his ashes soon.

Now I was left alone.

My birth parents had died before I had had a chance to really know them, and my adoptive parents had died when I still needed them. The only man close to me was Marc, but I didn't want to see him because we would end up having sex just like every time we met.

Sex was no longer a priority for me, but in a way, I missed it. I missed the nights I went from bed to bed so I wouldn't have to fall asleep. I haven't slept at night since I had that nightmare about Miguel. I was afraid I would do something wrong to someone, especially after discovering that those crimes in my dreams had been real.

All the crimes had been real except the one involving Miguel. If I had killed all of those people in my dreams, why was Miguel still alive? Was he going to help me get rid of my torments? Was he my salvation, or would he put an end to my suffering?

After the divorce was final and I moved to my new apartment, I started investigating those cases myself. I contacted the same detective I had paid to look for my parents. I couldn't handle it alone, and I couldn't risk going to the places where the murders had been committed. I couldn't risk Miguel finding out I was investigating the cases.

I had to find out the truth.

I needed to know why I had killed those people, and I needed to find out everything before Kalmin came back to me. I didn't want to lose the peace he offered when he was around me. I didn't want to lose him, and I wasn't ready to face life alone.

After three days, I received an envelope from the detective. He told me that in the envelope was everything he had discovered. He said it had been complicated for him to find the information I had asked for.

I put the envelope on the table. I sat on the couch and looked at it. I was afraid to open it. I was worried that what I would find would change me forever.

I don't know exactly how long it was until I dared to open the envelope. The first case I opened was the one with the little girl who had been killed.

I hoped this would be the last.

I left the picture on the table and turned it upside down. I couldn't look at her anymore. It hurt a lot because I had killed a child. My birth father's name was in that file. The little girl I had killed apparently was his ex-wife's daughter. My father had told me that she could not have children, and yet she had had three children.

When I saw them all sleeping, I remembered when I opened the door to the bedroom where a teenager slept and then the door to the bedroom where the little ones slept. Still, why did I have to kill that little girl?

Why didn't I kill her mother?

What was the fault of that child? Why did that child have to pay for the woman who had cursed my mother?

The older woman I had crucified on the ceiling was the head of the orphanage where I had lived for five years. A particular picture caught my eye. It was a photo from when I was a child, and when she had been younger. I remembered the nightmare in which a black shadow had entered my body. She had been the woman pulling me by my hand down that long, creepy hallway and throwing me into that red room.

The man I'd had sex with and killed was the son of a businessman from my father's company.

A memory came flooding back. I think I had been seven at the time. My father's driver had picked me up from school and brought me to his office. My father had promised me that we would eat together and spend the whole day in the city that day. When I got to his office, he wasn't there.

He had a conference call. His secretary told me he would finish quickly, so I sat down in his chair and waited. When the door opened, I thought it was my father, but it was one of his business partners. He closed the door behind him and came toward me.

He started stroking me.

It seemed strange to me.

He took off my panties and raped me before I could resist. I wanted to scream, but he put his hand to my mouth. He threatened to kill my father if I told him anything. He had probably killed my parents when the plane had crashed even though I had never said anything about that day.

The woman who had several wounds on her body had been found dead in an orphanage, the same one I had grown up in. She was the one who ran the orphanage at the time and was one of the two women in that red room. She had enchanted the demon that had possessed me.

I was shocked.

All the pictures were scattered on the table. I looked at them and cried. Those people may have deserved to die, but why was I supposed to be their killer?

There were two people still alive.

The second woman in the red room and Miguel.

Were they my next victims? I was terrified. I didn't want to kill anyone, and I didn't want to live with so many crimes on my conscience. But it was weird that part of me was rejoicing over those crimes. Part of me wanted more blood, more torn souls.

-The Hell of Depression-
They say that Hell is crowded, yet,

when you're in Hell,

you always seem to be alone.

& you can;t tell anyone when you're in Hell

or they'll think you're crazy

& being crazy is being in Hell

& being sane is hellish too.

Those who escape Hell, however,

never talk about it

& nothing much bothers them after that.

- Kaustubh Deshmukh -

CHAPTER 19

One night I fell asleep. I had resisted so sleeping at night for so long that I was exhausted. I couldn't sleep much during the day either, so I had started working for the company that my adoptive father had left me. I had to get involved with the business before it went bankrupt.

Marc had started taking money from the company, money he couldn't explain in any way. He was probably putting it into an account to secure his future. I couldn't afford to fire him because I still needed him. He knew how to handle the company better than I did, and I didn't have time to look for someone as good as him.

The night I fell asleep, I had the strangest and most horrible nightmare. I woke up in an ancient room. The walls looked older than the world. A few candles were lit around me, and I was lying on something very high. I wanted to get up and get down, but I couldn't move.

My body was inert.

I noticed that I was wearing a red dress, or so it seemed. It was made of a strange material that I had never seen before. Everything around me was strange and unknown. I had never seen such a room before. Not even in my dreams.

I heard the door open, but I couldn't see in which direction it was. I could hear footsteps approaching me. I began to feel an incredible fear. I almost fainted when Kalmin appeared next to me.

It was not possible.

It couldn't be true.

First my husband and now Kalmin?

He started stroking my hand. He started with the fingers of my right hand and trailed them up to my neck. He made a strange mark on my neck that I could not understand and then touched my face. He caressed me with the same tenderness as when we'd made love.

It couldn't be true.

I had to wake up from this nightmare before doing anything I would later regret. Kalmin made another strange sign with his finger on my forehead. This time, too, I couldn't understand what kind of movement it was. I wanted to ask him what he was doing there and what he would do to me, but I couldn't talk.

My lips moved, but no sound came out.

He put his finger to my mouth and motioned for me to be quiet. His chest was bare. Instead of pants, he wore another strange material.

He climbed up next to me and started kissing me. He removed the straps from my dress and kissed me on the shoulders. He caressed my whole body. The pleasure I had once felt with him had now turned into terror and fear.

At one point, he got up and stood over me. Kalmin had turned into a demon. A red demon with golden eyes that shone so brightly I couldn't look at him.

He was a beautiful demon.

He was the same demon I had seen the last night before I separated from Miguel, the same one Miguel had seen.

He didn't look like the other demons I'd seen before then. He didn't look like a monster. He had a man's red body and the face of a demon that didn't look like it was going to hurt me. He started talking.

His voice was calm and gentle.

I think that scared me the most. A demon couldn't have such a gentle voice. The demon told me that he had been waiting for me long enough, and it was time to come and take me to his world.

He told me that I did not belong to this world and that I belonged to him.

At that moment, I woke up scared. I was in my apartment. It was still night. I started to cry. I could still feel the demon's hands on my body. I could still hear his voice in my head, and I could still hear his words. I wasn't ready to die. I wasn't prepared to be possessed by that demon.

I couldn't figure out what he was going to do to me. I had to find the witch who had enchanted the demon to save me from Abyzou. I needed to know what the Hell I was struggling with and what he would do to me.

Was Kalmin that demon?

Is that why he'd came into my life unexpectedly and had stayed even though he knew I was married? Even though he knew my life wasn't normal like other people's?

He had promised to come see me in two days. Would that be the end of my life? Was he the demon who had possessed me all my life?

But then who were the other demons, and what did they want from me?

Why did others appear and disappear?

What was going on with me?

I had so many questions, and I didn't know where to look for the answers. I had begun to be afraid of Kalmin, and I didn't know if I should tell him to cancel his trip to come to me or let him come. I wanted to be wrong, and I wanted that nightmare to be just a nightmare.

If my ex-husband had escaped from my nightmare with his life, maybe I was wrong about Kalmin, too. Perhaps he had appeared in my dream because I miss him so much. Perhaps I had dreamed of him because I miss him and the peace his presence offered me.

Is that why I felt so calm when I was in his arms? Could that be the reason I could sleep next to him without having nightmares? The only nightmare I had that first night I'd slept with Kalmin was about my childhood, about the night when a demon entered my body. Was that a sign?

Had his very presence next to me caused that nightmare? Did my husband have to die so the demon could take me?

The Sun was beginning to rise, and I was still crying and thinking about everything that had happened to me lately. I tried to find an explanation or any answers to my questions. I opened my laptop to look for a witch.

I needed one to uncover the mysteries that drove me crazy. I needed the witch who had sold me to the demon who possessed me to save my life from Abyzou's clutches. I didn't know where to look for her. I didn't know anything about her, but I would go to all the witches I could find. I was sure that the one who had the answers to my questions would recognize me when she saw me.

*One day you'll make peace with
your demons, and the chaos in
your heart will settle flat.
and maybe for the first time in your life, life will
smile right
back at you and welcome you home.
- R.M. Drake -*

CHAPTER 20

I was determined to find the witch who could give me answers before Kalmin came to me. I wanted to make sure he wasn't the demon that had haunted me all my life. I had two days to find her.

On the first day, I was not successful. The witches I went to seemed to have no idea what was happening to me. They probably weren't real witches, and they probably had no power if they weren't able to see the demon or demons in me.

I didn't even know if there were several demons or if there was only one left. I could only see them if I looked in the mirror or at something that reflected my face. I had tried as much as possible to avoid mirrors and everything that looked like a mirror.

I couldn't even drive anymore because I was afraid that I would only see demons when I looked in the rearview mirror. When I went to work, I used the stairs so I wasn't left alone in the elevator. The interior consisted only of mirrors.

I wasted most of the next day looking for the right witch. Toward evening, a few hours before Kalmin would reach me, I entered a building that seemed familiar.

A young woman was sitting in a dark room at a table full of candles. She motioned for me to sit down. She had a strange object in her hand that seemed ancient.

She began saying something in a language unknown to me and started walking around me. In her other hand, she held a candle out of which came a red, fragrant smoke; the scent was strange but pleasant.

This peculiar ceremony went on longer than I thought. I didn't understand what the witch was doing to me or what she wanted to do to me.

"I had to cast out the demon that came with you so we could talk," she said when she finished.

I was speechless when I heard what she said. It seemed I had finally found the right witch to solve the mystery. I was fascinated that she could see the demon, and I was happy to have answers before I met up with Kalmin.

"My mother died two years ago, but before she died, she told me you would come here. I didn't know what you were going to look like, but I knew you were going to have a demon with you.

"My mother told me that your parents came to her before you were born and begged her to save you. Your only chance at life was to be sold to a demon, the most powerful demon that exists and has ever existed.

"My mother tried to explain to your parents that what they wanted to do was extremely dangerous and that when she opened the gates of

Hell to summon the demon that would possess you, other demons might come out and try to kill you and to destroy you. Your parents knew the risks, and yet they agreed.

"When you turn thirty-five, the demon will come take you because you do not belong to this world. You came here today with only one demon. It means that this demon has managed to defeat the others with your help.

"You were so strong that you managed to cast them away, and you did not allow them to take control of you. The name of the demon that possesses you is Caligor. He is the king of the Hell into which assassins and people who commit depraved deeds are thrown."

"In one month, I will be thirty-five years old. Will I die in a month?"

"You will not die. You cannot die. You are immortal. When the demon Caligor was summoned, you became immortal. That's why you have managed to defeat the other demons. You are a demon in a woman's body. You are the bride of the demon Caligor, and that is why he will take you with him. This demon doesn't want to hurt you. He loves you and has always protected you so you would reach a human age mature enough for him to take you with him.

"Unfortunately, I can't help you nor do I think there is anything that can be done to make the demon Caligor give up on you."

I started crying.

I needed answers, but I was not prepared for such a solution. I could not accept that I was a demon, and I could not accept that I would no longer exist in this world in a month.

My phone keeps ringing.

It is Kalmin.

He had arrived in Manhattan and needed my address. I wasn't ready to see him yet. I gave him the address and called the man at the front desk to give him the key to let him into the apartment.

I left the witch's room with a broken soul. I walked the streets without knowing where to go. It was already dark outside.

It was darker than ever.

I had an hour left until the witch's spell was shattered and the demon Caligor would appear next to me again. I had another hour of freedom and peace, and I didn't know what I wanted to do. I thought of committing suicide, but what if the witch was right and I was immortal? I was confused and in pain.

I loved Kalmin very much, and I didn't want to leave this world. I didn't want to be the bride of that demon. I couldn't stand the thought. I was not ready to leave this world even though I had never found my place among the people. Now I had a reason to want to stay here.

Then she loved him as she would a manifestation of herself, both silenced and wounded in existence, both everything and nothing to eternity.
- E.J. Koh -

CHAPTER 21

I went home. I knew I wouldn't find a solution soon. My mind was too tired and full of too much information. I knew Kalmin was waiting for me, and I was eager to feel the peace he offered me again. I didn't know if I could trust him after that horrible nightmare, but I was going to enjoy his presence as much as possible. Soon, I would no longer exist in this world, and I did not want to imagine what awaited me beyond it.

I couldn't even put the key in the door to unlock it because Kalmin opened it for me. I was amazed that he felt me coming.

My house was completely different.

Colored lights illuminated the room. Scented candles and flowers of all colors delighted my eyes and senses. Dinner was ready. Steam was coming from the food on the living room table. He was still standing in front of the door. I couldn't even utter a word of astonishment.

No one had ever cared this much for me. I had never received such attention from a man. Kalmin didn't look like the kind of man to make such gestures and amazed me every time we met.

I had the most beautiful night of my life.

Did Kalmin know that he would never see me again, or did he know that my life in this world would end soon? Was that why he wanted to pamper me so much? Was he the demon whose bride I was to become and wanted to make my last days in this world memorable?

I wished I could ask him, but if I was just paranoid and he was only a simple man, should I tell him everything about my miserable life in this world? How would he react if I told him I was immortal? What would he do if he found out that I would become the bride of a demon and disappear from this world as if I had never existed?

I asked him to stay with me that night, and I was amazed when he told me that he wanted move in with me. I was happy that I would at least have the most beautiful four weeks of my life.

Even though they were my last days in this world, I was determined to make them as beautiful as possible. I took Kalmin to my company that I was trying so hard to get back. I introduced him to Marc and told him about the fraud he was perpetrating in the company.

Kalmin promised to help me with everything I needed to be able to report Marc. If he succeeded, I intended to put him in charge. He was already better prepared than I was in the business world, and I was sure he would get the company out of bankruptcy.

We went out every night for dinner. We walked through the park every day. We went every weekend for a picnic or camping in a tent. The days passed quickly, and I was happier than ever. I had no more nightmares.

I no longer saw demons in the mirror.

I could no longer feel any invisible presences around me. It was the first time that I saw life with different eyes. It was the first time I learned how to live in this world. It was the first time I had known happiness and love in all its possible forms. Now more than ever, I wanted to stay in this world.

I wanted to live here with Kalmin.

I still had a lot to learn.

I still had a lot of love to offer.

I had love I had never felt before.

All sorts of beautiful feelings surrounded every cell of my body. I was delighted. Kalmin made me happier and became more and more protective of me every day. He protected me from any obstacles that stood in my way. Sometimes he even protected me from me.

He knew me better than I did. However, I had been so selfish that I had never asked him about his life, his past. It was enough for me to know the man he is now. All he had to offer me now was enough.

I was not yet ready to learn more about his life, and I hoped to have more time. I hoped that our love would save me from Caligor's clutches.

I wanted that demon to disappear from my life and let me be happy in this world because this time I was really happy. Now I wanted to be able to live. Now I had reasons to stay in this world.

I would find a way to save souls while eradicating demons from this world. I'd find a way to save my own soul. I just had to. ... I could only hope.
- Ketley Allison -

CHAPTER 22

Five weeks after my divorce, and just a day before my birthday, I received a message from Miguel. He told me he wanted us to meet at the vacation home we had on Duck Island. He said he needed to talk to me urgently and he was already there.

I didn't understand what could be so urgent that it couldn't wait until he returned to Manhattan. It was strange that he wanted to meet me the day before my birthday, the day before the demon Caligor would come to take me from this world.

Was Miguel the demon?

Wasn't that why I killed him in my nightmare? Everything was becoming more and more mysterious. Kalmin did not want to let me go alone, but I assured him that I would be safe. I would not allow Miguel to harm me. I couldn't die anyway, so I wasn't afraid of anyone or anything.

I had begun to like the idea that I was immortal, but I couldn't get used to the idea that I would have to be the bride of a demon and that I would soon be out of this world.

I was still trying to find a way to stay in this world. I continued to hope that the demon would leave me alone and maybe find someone else. There had to be a solution, and I kepy trying to find it up until the last moment.

I went to the vacation home that very day. I hadn't been there in a few years. I still hadn't decided if I would leave it to Miguel or keep it. It had been my adoptive parents' vacation home, and I didn't really need anything to remind me of them. I didn't want to remember them after learning from my birth father that they hadn't let my mother see me.

Now more than ever, I wanted my parents who had given me life alive. I knew that only they would understand my pain and only they would understand what I was going through.

I arrived at the vacation home in the evening. Miguel was waiting for me on the porch in front of the house with an almost empty bottle of wine.

I poured some wine into a glass and sat down next to him. We started talking about our marriage. I hoped that hadn't been why he had called me there.

I wasn't going to go back to him. I didn't feel anything for him anymore. I don't even think I'd ever loved him. I think I married him just because he was different from the other men I'd been with before. And yet, our marriage had lasted a long time, probably because I was too busy fighting the demons trying to control me.

At length, he got up and brought another bottle of wine. I had a feeling that something terrible was going to happen. I felt like he needed more alcohol to tell me why he had called me there. After we drank the second bottle of wine together, he got up and took my hand.

We went for a walk.

There were a lot of trees around the house, but also a lot of lights. It was a superb vacation home—an oasis of relaxation for getting away from a stressful week at work.

We walked to the edge of the hill on which the house sat. It was darker there, and I've always been afraid to go there. Down beneath the hill was the sea. That evening the wind blew with power.

I could hear the waves crashing against the rocks on the shore. There is no beach there. It was the only place on the island where there was no beach. Instead, it was full of very sharp and dangerous rocks.

When I reached the edge of the hill, I had the feeling that something terrible was going to happen to me.

Miguel was very quiet, and I thought perhaps he was crying, but I couldn't see his face very well in the darkness.

We started arguing. Miguel started talking about the crimes he was investigating. I didn't quite understand why he he was screaming at me and not speaking very coherently.

He grabbed me by the shoulders and shook me. He kept telling me that I was an assassin. That I was a monster and that I killed those people. How was it possible for him to know all this? I tried to release myself from his grip.

He hurt me.

My shoulders and my whole body ached. Miguel pushed me more and more toward the edge of the cliff. Was he going to kill me? Was that why he had called me here? Could he not bear the thought of living with a criminal for so many years?

I tried to explain everything to him, that I wasn't the one doing the killing, but he didn't want to listen to me.

I tried hard to get away from him.

My leg slipped, and Miguel pushed me, throwing me into the abyss without a trace of regret.

The man I had lived with under the same roof and who always said he loved me had just thrown me into the abyss. He was going to kill me in cold blood without giving me a chance to explain to him what happened. I flailed my hands in the air and begged for help.

My hair covered my face.

I could see Miguel kneeling on the edge of the precipice looking down at me. The moment of impact on the rocks was excruciating. I wanted to scream in pain, but I had no voice. Tears streamed down my face. I could feel their wet warmth enveloping my face. I couldn't see Miguel anymore.

It was completely dark.

My body hung stuck on a rock, and yet I lived. I felt unbearable pain, but I was still alive.

Apparently the witch had been right when she'd said I was immortal. I closed my eyes. I wanted to die.

Then I felt someone sitting on top of me. It was the same beautiful demon whose bride I was supposed to become.

Caligor had come to take me.

He had enormous wings.

His wings were red with tips as golden as his eyes. The golden tips illuminated the place where I was. He gently pulled me off the top of the cliff and took me in his arms. He put a hand on my wound.

The wound started to heal.

I felt no more pain. I felt powerful instead. I felt like I was getting stronger and stronger. Caligor rose into the air with me still in his arms. He rose until he reached the edge of the precipice where Miguel was still kneeling.

When he saw us, he fell on his back. Then Caligor went down, and we both disappeared into the sea.

"I am being murdered by my own mind."
"They left me alone with my thoughts, and my thoughts ate me alive."

CHAPTER 23

MIGUEL

I had worked day and night to investigate the recent crimes.

I called Melissa to the vacation home because I knew it was the only place we could talk without interruption. I knew that at that time of year, there was no one on the island. It was too cold here for vacation.

Melissa had divorced me because I didn't have time to be her husband, because I didn't have time to spend my nights or vacations with her, but she didn't know how many sacrifices I had had to make to become such a good detective. She probably didn't know that I still loved her even though I wasn't always present in her life. I loved her like I had never loved a woman.

I missed her very much after she'd left. I know it was mostly my fault, but she hadn't even wanted to give me a second chance to fix everything. Or maybe she had given me more opportunities than she should have. Even though I now had someone else in my life, I still loved Melissa.

I was going to sell the house she had left me after the divorce. I didn't want to live there either. I wanted to start a new life with a woman who understood me more than Melissa. I had even bought a new house and started moving my things there.

When I let Melissa know that I would be selling the house, she was not at all surprised.

She didn't even want to accept any money from the sale of the house.

Most of our things, especially those that reminded me of Melissa, I took to a storage warehouse. I hadn't been in the basement in a long time. I didn't even know what was there anymore, but I had to empty the house so I could sell it. One day I went down to see what I could keep and what I had to throw away.

I found many old things down there that had to be thrown away; some things I had never even seen before and some I didn't even need.

As I climbed the stairs to go back up, I stumbled and leaned against a wall. A brick fell from it.

Inside was a red box.

I was surprised to see secret holes in the wall. It was too new and modern of a building for such hiding places to be normal. I took out the box and went up to the living room. I put the box on the table and looked in it.

I had a hunch.

I wouldn't like what I'd find inside.

I sat down in the chair, and, without overthinking it, I opened the box. Inside the box were weapons, and I knew right away they were the weapons used at the crimes we were investigating.

I found the corkscrew used to kill the young man. I found the knife used to kill the woman. I found the missing chain from the cross of the older woman I'd found hanging from the ceiling. I found the bracelet missing from the hand of the murdered girl.

At the bottom of the box, I found my wedding ring that I thought I had lost. I woken up one morning without a wedding ring on my finger, and I thought I'd lost it somewhere. I'd looked for it everywhere, and I had never found it.

All of this pointed to the mystery I hadn't been able to unravel no matter how long I worked on those cases.

I got up and went to my office to look for the case files. I took them back to the living room and placed every object next to the corresponding file. They all fit perfectly with the forensic descriptions.

I didn't know what to think.

I was so confused. I didn't know what to do with the weapons and the other objects noted as missing from the crime scenes.

Everything felt evil. It seemed to be related to a cult or something demonic. Had Melissa committed those crimes?

What reasons would she have to do it?

Was that why she had been so sick all the time?

Could she not sleep at night because of this?

Because I wasn't certain she had committed the crimes and didn't want to accuse her unjustly, I took those items into the precinct to be investigated. I asked a close friend to check for fingerprints on the objects and tell the results only to me. Before officially handing them over to the police, I wanted to know if they even matched Melissa's.

I don't even know if I would have been able to hand them over. It would have meant Melissa would go to jail, and I didn't think I wanted her put there. I still loved her and wanted to protect her.

Her birthday was approaching.

I wanted to spend time with her.

So I texted her to meet me at the vacation home. I got there a few hours before her, wanting to prepare a surprise. I was in the kitchen preparing dinner when I heard the phone ring. I was hoping it wouldn't be Melissa telling me she wasn't coming. By the time I got to the phone that I'd left in the living room, it had stopped ringing.

I saw on the screen that I had a voicemail from my friend who was running the fingerprints. I was reluctant to listen to that message. I didn't want to spoil the surprise for Melissa, but at the same time, I wanted to know the results.

I wanted and hoped that the results would be negative. I mustered up my courage and listened to the message. I dropped the phone when I learned that the fingerprints matched. It couldn't be true. I was devastated.

Black smoke enveloped the room. My food had burned.

I threw everything in the trash.

I opened a bottle of wine and went to the terrace to think. I didn't know what to do.

By the time Melissa arrived, I had drunk almost all of the wine in the bottle. I watched as Melissa poured the remaining wine into her own glass. I didn't dare to tell her what I had found out.

I didn't know how she would react, and I started becoming afraid of her. I had found my wedding ring in that box, so I didn't know what she was going to do to me. I began to regret having called her here and that we were now alone on this island.

She could kill me and throw me into the sea. No one would ever find me.

I asked her to go for a walk with me. I was losing my patience, and I had to have the courage to tell her I knew the truth.

When we moved away from the house and fell prey to the darkness, I started screaming at her. I started telling her everything I knew. I didn't give her a chance to say anything because what she told me didn't make sense. Nothing made sense anymore. I grabbed her by the shoulders.

I felt an incredible hatred for her.

The darkness gave me incredible strength to face her.

I didn't realize we were on the edge of the cliff. I only realized it when Melissa tried to break away from my hands and fell down deep into the dark abyss. I knelt to try to see her. It was very dark, but I could see her. Her body lay stuck on a rock. I had killed her.

Regret began to take up root in my heart. I hadn't planned on killing Melissa. I don't know what happened to me in that moments. I wasn't me anymore. It was as if someone else had taken control of me and my reason.

I stayed standing on the edge of the precipice and shouting at her, hoping to hear her.

I hoped she was alive.

Then suddenly a monster with enormous wings appeared in front of me. The demon was holding Melissa in his arms.

I fell on my back and was paralyzed with fear. I could not react. I don't even remember what happened after that. I just remember waking up at the police station in an interrogation room with handcuffs on my wrists.

Demons are demons, and if you have them, you can either put them away, exorcize them, or carry them with you.

- Jill Flint -

CHAPTER 24

KALMIN

Melissa had not returned home as promised, and now it was her birthday. I had planned several surprises for her. I called her, but she didn't answer. I had even called Miguel, but he didn't answer either. It was strange.

I went to Melissa's company to pick up the helicopter from the roof of the building.

I had to get to her as soon as possible.

I had promised Melissa that I would always take care of her and always protect her. I was going to keep my word just like I was going to keep my word when I promised my wife I would protect her. I was young then, but I always kept my promises.

Except for that night.

That damn night.

I stayed at work overtime.

I had promised my wife that I would be home in time to take her to the hospital. She was in pain when she called me. I had something urgent to resolve that could not be postponed. I thought I would get home on time, but I was two hours late.

When I got home, my wife was lying by the stairs. There was so much blood around her. She had probably fallen down the stairs. She was still alive. I took her to the hospital immediately.

When I got to the hospital with her, she was in shock. She had begun to tremble, and blood was flowing from her mouth.

I waited for three hours to receive news from the doctors who were trying to save her life. Unfortunately, nothing could be done for her or our child. The baby had died when she'd fallen down the stairs.

I still regret not coming home when she had begged me, when she'd cried on the phone and told me she was in unbearable pain. I don't know what had been on my mind back then.

I still have nightmares in the night that I hold my baby in my arms and my wife appears out of nowhere covered in blood and takes my baby in her arms and kills him. It's been six years, and I still haven't forgiven myself because I loved my job more than my family. I lost my family because of my arrogance.

I wouldn't be able to forgive myself this time either if I had allowed something to happen to Melissa.

I arrived on the island and went to Melissa's vacation home. I could not enter the house, but I saw two bottles of wine and two glasses on the table of the terrace.

I thought maybe they had gone out somewhere, but then I saw the police tape on the front door. I heard voices behind me. Guided by the voices, I left and went toward the alley of the house.

There were a lot of cops in front of me.

I was walking, and I could feel my legs shaking.

A cop stopped me.

He told me I couldn't go forward. I told him I was Melissa's boyfriend and motioned to a police chief I knew to let me pass.

When I got to him, he put his hand on my shoulder and told me he was sorry. He said that Melissa and Miguel had had an argument last night, and Melissa had fallen into the abyss.

I went to the edge of the precipice.

Her blood had not yet been washed away by the crashing waves. A policeman approached and told me that they had not yet found her body. I didn't know what the chances were for her survival, but I still had hope.

I love her.

I love her and want her back in my life.

I found out that Miguel was the main suspect. Even though he said it had been an accident, I believed he pushed her.

I went to Melissa's apartment. I started drinking. I wanted to get drunk so I wouldn't feel the pain tearing my heart apart.

I wanted to take my heart out of my chest so I wouldn't suffer anymore. I hadn't even had the chance to tell Melissa how much I loved her.

I drank and I cried. Through the tears, I saw the black box that hid a ring with which I was going to ask Melissa to marry me. This was the second time I hadn't been able to protect who I loved most. It was the second time I'd lost what I most needed.

I didn't know how many days I drank and cried. I didn't know how long it had been since I'd seen Melissa for the last time. I didn't know anything anymore. I felt worse and worse from the alcohol.

I wanted to come back to have the strength to go and look for Melissa. I couldn't accept that she was dead.

She couldn't be dead.

I could feel her around me.

I felt that she needed me.

I went to the bathroom to vomit. I wanted to get all the alcohol out of me. I was lying on the floor when I saw something near the trash. I reached out my hand. It was a pregnancy test, a positive pregnancy test.

Was Melissa pregnant?

This was not possible.

Everything couldn't happen exactly like the first time. It was not possible to lose another child.

I went down to the police station. I wanted to know more about Melissa's case. The police chief called me into his office. He told me they still hadn't found her body. He said everything was a mystery. Miguel seemed to have gone mad. He kept repeating that a monster had taken Melissa into the sea.

He was now in a clinic.

I couldn't talk to him.

He had been sedated because he was punching himself in the head and repeating those same words over and over when he was awake. I didn't know what those words meant, but I was going to find out.

In the meantime, I fired Marc. I had enough evidence to denounce him. At least I was going to keep that promise to Melissa. I failed to recover the money Marc had stolen, but I would strive to double Melissa's income. I wanted her to be the richest woman in America when she returned. I wanted Melissa to be proud of me. I started taking care of her company as I had promised. I worked almost nonstop.

At night I slept on the office couch. It was hard for me to go to Melissa's apartment. I felt like I saw her everywhere, and sometimes I felt like I heard her shouting my name. I felt like she needed my help, but I didn't know what to do to help her and bring her back. I was devastated by the pain, but I wasn't going to give up. I was going to do whatever it took to get Melissa back.

TO BE CONTINUED...

Note From the Author

The idea for this book came to me in the first months I started to have insomnia. When I couldn't sleep, I started writing down what was going through my mind and what I was feeling.

Certain parts of the book are part of my life.

Certain feelings in the book are shown precisely as I felt them then.

At first, it was hard for me to accept that I had insomnia. I didn't understand why I couldn't sleep at night. I got angry, and sometimes I even started crying.

It was very frustrating, and I was jealous of my family members that could sleep so well and peacefully. They did not understand me, and even today, no one understands me. Sometimes I am afraid when the darkness swallows the light of day.

Sometimes I feel fearful when I want to sleep. Sometimes I'm scared to sleep. I am afraid that if I fall asleep, I will never be able to wake up again. I am worried that the darkness of the night will swallow me, and I will remain captive in another world.

The scene with the devil above Melissa is a real scene from my life. Many years ago, I went to the bedroom to sleep one night at almost midnight. I was alone in the apartment. It wasn't the first night I had slept alone, but it was the last night I slept in the dark. It was the last night I was going to sleep peacefully.

I don't know why it was that night, and I don't even remember what day or what month it was nor the year. It happened many years ago. I only know that at that time I was in Italy. I don't remember when I fell asleep or if I fell asleep, but suddenly I began to hear someone snoring next to me. At first, I didn't realize what was happening.

I didn't know if it was a dream or reality.

I began to hear the snoring louder and louder as if it was approaching me. I was paralyzed by fear. I wanted to get out of bed to turn on the light. I knew I was alone in the bedroom and alone in the apartment. I was the only human being in that apartment. No one could be snoring next to me.

Everything seemed so real.

Unfortunately, I couldn't move. I was so scared that I wanted to cry. Fear was all I felt. I could no longer feel my hands; I could no longer feel my legs. I could not react in any way. Instead, I continued hearing the snoring near my ear.

At one point, I thought it could be something demonic. I believed in God then, so if God could exist, then the devil could also exist. At least my brain was still working.

I wanted to raise my hand to make the sign of the cross.

That's how I knew I could cast the devil away, or so I had heard. I struggled repeatedly to move my hand, but I couldn't. That's when I remembered that I could make a cross with my tongue. The important thing was being able to make a cross.

My tongue was as paralyzed as my body.

I tried harder and harder and didn't give up until I could move my tongue. I managed to make the sign of the cross a few times. I don't know how many crosses I managed to make before I no longer heard the snoring. At last, it was quiet around me, and yet I still couldn't move my body. I continued to make the sign of the cross with my tongue.

At one point, I saw a shadow above me. It resembled the devil as described in the Bible and in many books. It was a black shadow with red horns and a long tail.

He grabbed my hands. I felt him hold my hands and hold me like that for a few moments. I felt those long-fingered hands on mone. I cannot express in words the fear that overwhelmed me at that moment. I continued to make the sign of the cross with my tongue until the devil was gone.

I began to feel my body again.

I quickly got out of bed.

I turned on all the lights in the apartment and looked for a cross. I took it in my hands and went to the living room to sit on the couch.

When I looked at the clock, it was midnight. It all had lasted only a few minutes or a few seconds. I don't know how long I needed to fall asleep or if I had fallen asleep at all. All I know is that when I went to bed, it had been almost midnight.

I pulled my legs close to my body and put my arms around my legs. I held the cross in my hands and cried. I cried so hard like a small child. I was crying out of fear. I cried until about four in the morning. I can't remember if I slept that morning, but I know that since then, for many years, I haven't slept in the dark.

Sometimes I couldn't sleep at night. Since then, I have not slept at night without saying a prayer and making the sign of the cross. I was terrified and horrified that he might return.

He came back many times. Sometimes when I wanted to sleep at lunch, strange and inexplicable things happened to me. Shortly after I went to bed, I didn't know if I was asleep or awake; everything got dark in the bedroom.

I was paralyzed with fear, and I couldn't move.

Sometimes I saw shadows approaching me; other times, I saw shadows sitting above me; most of the time, I woke up when the shadows touched my hands. I was always terrified. It was something that could not be explained in words, but I felt fear.

One evening, a few years after meeting the devil, I had a much more horrible nightmare than that. I know for sure this time I was sleeping, even if everything seemed real. I dreamed that there was a vast black hole around my bed. Its end could not be seen, but it began at the edge of my bed. Then I felt someone grab me by the leg.

I couldn't see who it was because it was as black as the hole he was pulling me into. I tried to resist and hold on to the bed so I wouldn't fall into that hole. I think I was aware that if I went into that black hole, I would have stayed there forever or probably would have died in real life.

The hand was pulling me harder and harder.

I had already reached the edge of the bed when I started screaming for help. At least, I was trying to scream for help, but I couldn't really yell. I don't know if I can explain this experience in words so you can fully understand it. I continued to scream until I thought I was screaming in real life, too.

I was starting to hear my voice, but I was no longer aware of whether everything that was happening to me was a dream or reality.

All I know is that at one point, a roommate heard me and came to me. He was trying to wake me up, but I couldn't because I was almost in that black hole. I kept my hands on the edge of the bed and kept screaming for help.

After a few minutes, he managed to wake me up and I realized that I was raising my hands, asking for help. After making contact with reality, I started to cry. I think I was crying while I had that horrible experience too because I felt tears on my face. It was the most frightening experience I had ever had with the darkness or maybe with the demons that I always felt haunted me.

I've had these weird experiences all my life. In all my dreams, whether they were good or nightmares, it is always dark. A darkness so strange that I could still see through. Since I was a child, I have felt that someone was looking at me in the dark. That someone was following me all the time.

I always felt like someone was still behind me. I often heard someone calling my name when, in fact, there was no one around me. Many people claim that they have had seen ghosts or have had the impression that they see ghosts.

I believe I met the devil himself and probably many other demons from Hell. But I'm not sure if everything that happened to me was real or just nightmares.

What is certain is that I felt everything as if it were real. I saw everything as if I existed in two parallel worlds. I have never felt like a normal person. I have always had dreams that later happened in real life. I have always had the feeling that I exist in several worlds at the same time.

Now I don't believe in God anymore. I don't believe in anything anymore. I don't believe in myself most of the time either. I no longer say my prayers when I have been sleeping for more than a year. I am no longer afraid of anyone or anything. And yet, with the loss of my faith in God, the strange moments in my life disappeared.

I no longer feel any presence around me. I can't hear my name anymore. I have no more nightmares in which the demons want to possess me.

I'm just afraid of the dark.

Darkness remains my greatest fear.

I will probably get rid of this fear just as I got rid of the others. Now I've become just like Melissa, a sad, desperate, lonely woman. A person who lives every day only with the hope that maybe it will be the last day.

I have just become a package of meat and bones.

A human body that no longer has the life or energy to fight the daily challenges.

A lost and sad soul, a heart that screams for love and peace.

I still have insomnia.

ABOUT THE AUTHOR

I forgot about myself.... How long it took me to realize that the most important person in my life is ME!

I was busy being always present for others, always attentive to the needs of others, willing to give everything and not refuse anyone. Those who know me can confirm or deny what is written and what will follow...

I was busy pleasing everyone, helping and thanking everyone. Later I noticed that there were too few who tried to please me.

I was busy giving, sharing everything I had so I would not receive anything in return. And moreover, when I had nowhere else to go, I was reproached and set aside, thrown away by those to whom I gave everything...

I was busy making people happy who did not know how to appreciate me.

I was busy cheering on others while my soul was crying.

I was busy receiving criticisms and reprimands for what I did and what I did not do, as if I was forced to do or not do something, as if others had the right to impose on me how to live my life.

I was busy being judged by some who believed themselves to be standards of ethics and morality.

I was busy enduring insults, blows to the back, betrayals, crises, and whims from people devoid of humanity and character.

I was busy waiting for appreciation from people who are incapable of recognizing merit.

I was busy suffering for those who did not deserve it and crying for some who built their happiness on my tears.

I was busy trying to show those unable to know me... what I really am.

I was busy peeling off labels, some of which stuck to me after the first impression.

I was busy making mistakes that I did not make and evaluating myself according to the "normality and values" of others.

I was busy wearing a mask for some people, who, if they had seen how I really am—a vulnerable, sensitive person—would not have stepped on my feet and would not have taken advantage of me.

I was busy letting others limit me.

I was busy enduring the envy of some and feeling guilty that I have more than them, defending those who lack personality and cowards—at the risk of making enemies—but I have not seen any of them ever defend me.

I was busy forgiving people who have wronged me.

I was busy proving to some that I was a good person, forgetting that those with wicked souls could not see others as good.

I was busy rejoicing in the achievements of others, suffering for their failures, and forgetting to rejoice in my own accomplishments or to weep for my own troubles.

I was busy listening to others, interested in their pain, their dreams, but too few showed that they cared about my sufferings and dreams.

I was busy dealing with the problems of others.

I was busy wasting my time with selfish, pessimistic people who charged me negatively and from whom I did not learn anything good.

I was busy waiting for others and postponing doing what I wanted, considering what others wanted and forgetting what I wanted.

I was busy adding and deleting priorities, dreams, and people from my list.

I was busy giving time from my only life to bolster some who only used me, to take care of the health of others, and to neglect my own health.

I was busy making efforts to teach them some good things I know, only to find that they only learned the bad parts from me.

I was busy educating others and forgot to educate myself.

I was busy trying to be perfect for people full of flaws.

I was busy lying and hiding to protect myself from the curious, from those who think you owe it to yourself to put your life on the table, and from those who judge lives and to justify myself in front of others for my actions and decisions.

I was busy paying attention to those around me, only to find that I was ignored.

I was busy loving people who I thought loved me, but who betrayed and forgot me, criticized, and judged instead of meeting new people.

I was busy decaying and degrading myself with those who dragged me after them.

I was busy educating my reason and ignoring my heart, having time for others and not having time for myself.

I was busy not forgetting about others, and I forgot about myself, living the lives of others, that I forgot to live my own life.

But that's it! That is enough! From now on I will be busy making a list of priorities, dreams, and plans.

I will be busy living only for myself and for those who truly deserve to be around me.

I will be busy learning that not everyone deserves my time and love.

I will be busy learning that I have the right to make choices at will and without consulting others.

I will be busy learning that I am not obliged to please everyone, and that it is not important for me to be accepted by everyone, especially by those who have absurd pretensions.

I will be busy recovering unfulfilled dreams, people I have become estranged from, things I have postponed doing when I was too busy to do what I like.

I will be busy not listening to criticism, not allowing anyone to blame me for anything, no longer responding to challenges, no longer letting myself be dragged down by those who do not respect themselves as people.

I will be busy refusing those who always want something from me.

I will be busy being me... the one I want to be, not the one others want me to be.

I will be busy fulfilling all my debts to myself, getting used to the idea that I have no obligations to others and that the only duty I have to people is respect.

I will be busy starting to forget my life and continuing with the little life I have left...

Printed in Great Britain
by Amazon

66748624R00139